MW01126597

LUCIAN
&
DAHLIA

WILLOW WINTERS &
LAUREN LANDISH
WALL STREET JOURNAL & USA TODAY BESTSELLING AUTHORS

From USA Today bestselling authors Willow Winters and Lauren Landish comes a sexy and forbidden series of standalone romances.

Everything has a price ... and I'm willing to pay.

I trust no one. I thrive with control and I've learned to be ruthless and cold-hearted. I'm not interested in love, but I still have desires.

That's where Dahlia comes in. She's never been a submissive before and I'm eager to train her. When I saw her on stage at the auction, dressed in gold, I knew I had to have her.

She was meant to be a distraction. Nothing more.

One lie changed everything. A lie she told to hide how broken she really is.

I own her for now. She's mine for an entire month. But a month isn't long enough for what I want to do with her. I don't care what the contract says. I bought her and now she's mine.

BOUGHT

PROLOGUE

LUCIAN

I slowly pace the room, letting the sound of my shoes clacking against the floor startle her. My eyes are on Dahlia, watching her every movement. Her breathing picks up as she realizes I've come back for her. With her blindfold on and her wrists and ankles tied to the bed while she lies on her belly, she's at my complete mercy, and she knows it.

The sight of her bound and waiting for me is so tempting. I force my groan back.

Her pale, milky skin is on full display as she waits for me. I've left her like this deliberately, in this specific position. She knows now not to move, not to struggle. She knows to wait for me obediently, and what's more, *she enjoys it*.

The wooden paddle gently grazes along her skin, leaving

goosebumps down her thigh in its wake. They trail up the curve of her ass, and her shoulders rise as she sucks in a breath. Her body tenses and her lips part, spilling a soft moan. She knows what's coming.

She's *earned* this.

She lied to me.

And she's going to be punished.

She doesn't know this is for her own good. She should, but she hasn't realized it yet.

I'm only doing this for her. She *needs* this.

She needs to heal, and I know just how to help her. The paddle whips through the air and smacks her lush ass, leaving a bright red mark as she gasps, her hands gripping the binds at her wrists. I watch as her pussy clenches around nothing, making my dick that much harder.

Soon.

I barely maintain my control and gently knead her ass, soothing the pulsing pain I know she's feeling. "Tell me why you lied to me, treasure," I whisper at the shell of her ear, my lips barely touching her sensitive skin.

"I'm sorry," she whimpers with lust. I don't want her apology. I want her to realize what she's done. I want to know why she hid it from me all this time. She'll learn she can't lie to me. There's no reason she should.

Smack! I bring the paddle down on the other cheek and her body jolts as a strangled cry leaves her lips, her pussy glistening with arousal.

"That's not what I asked, treasure." My tone is taunting. She needs to realize what I already know. She needs to admit it. To me, but mostly to herself.

I pull away from her, just for a moment, leaving her to writhe on the bed from the sting of the paddle.

I didn't anticipate our relationship reaching this point.

In the beginning, I thought this would be fun. Just a form of stress relief for me.

But things changed.

I bought her at auction, and now she can't leave. She's mine for an entire month. But the days have flown by, and the contract is almost over.

I need more time.

I'm going to make this right. I'm going to heal my treasure.

If it's the last thing I do, I'll give her what she needs. What we both need.

She parts those beautiful lips, and hope blooms in my chest.

Say it, tell me what you desperately need to say.

But her mouth closes, and she shifts slightly on the sheets before stilling and waiting patiently for more.

I pull my arm back and steady myself. Soon, she'll realize it. My broken treasure. Soon she'll be *healed*, but that won't be enough for me anymore. I want more.

Smack!

CHAPTER 1

LUCIAN

A FEW WEEKS PRIOR

I stare at my jacket, laying it over the arm of the tufted leather chair in the corner of my office. I need to leave this fucking building and get home, but I don't fucking want to. It's not like I have anything waiting for me. Nothing to do but more work.

I've spent a fortune on my home. I built it from the ground up, painstakingly choosing every piece of hardware and meticulously designing each room myself. But I couldn't give a damn if I go back there anymore.

It's cold and lifeless. Empty.

My brow furrows, and a frustrated sigh leaves my lips. I could keep working. *There's always more work waiting.*

I clench my jaw and type the password to unlock my computer, the gentle tapping of the keys soothing me. It's a comforting sound. But only for a moment.

As the screen lights up and I glance at the window of emails left on the desktop, I seethe and remember why I'm in such a horrible fucking mood. My eyes focus on the lawyer's name attached to the most recent email. This is why I'm so damn pissed and aggravated.

I'm fucking tired of leeches always suing me. Trying to take a piece of me they haven't earned. Most of the lawsuits don't bother me. It comes with the territory. But my *family,* and my *ex-wife?* It fucking shreds me, and I hate that I ever felt anything for them. At some point in time I had feelings for them, emotions I've long since grown cold to.

Now there's only anger.

I steady myself, knowing they've tried this before and failed. They'll keep trying, and it's aggravating, but I refuse to give them anything. I've learned my lesson the hard way. I know better now.

My eyes widen as a new email pops up.

From Club X.

It's been a long time since I've seen an email from Madam Lynn. And an even longer time since I've set foot into the club. The pad of my thumb rubs along the tips of both my middle finger and forefinger, itching to see what's inside.

Images flash before my eyes, and I can practically hear the

soft sounds of the whip smacking against flesh and a moan forced from the Submissive's lips. Never to hurt, only for pleasure. Whips aren't my tool of choice, nor what I've been known for in the past. But nonetheless, the memory kicks the corners of my lips up into a grin. I tap my fingers on the desk, debating on opening the message before moving the mouse over to the email and clicking on it out of curiosity.

Check your mail, sir.

I huff a laugh at the message and immediately hit the intercom button on my desktop phone for my secretary. It's not yet five, so she better fucking be at her desk still.

"Yes, Mr. Stone?" she responds, and her voice comes through with a sweet and casual air.

"Could you bring me my mail, please?" Although it's poised as a question, it isn't one. There's only one correct response, and she knows that.

There's no hesitation as Linda says, "Of course." Her voice is slightly raspy. Linda's old, to put it bluntly; she should retire.

If I was her I would, rather than putting up with my arrogant ass.

I'm happy she hasn't though. Every year I pay her more money to stay. A hefty raise, a gift here and there. It keeps her happy. Finding a good secretary is more work than it's worth. It was a pain in my ass when I started. Linda's the first I've been able to keep for more than two months and now that she knows what she's doing, with more than four years of working for me, I have no intention of finding a new secretary. So when I make a request, I say *please*.

I go through the emails remaining in my inbox, waiting impatiently for her soft knock on the door to my office. Usually I don't bother with the paper mail. Just like most of these fucking emails, they're junk. She knows what to do with them. So I leave it to her to organize and sift through it daily. She hands over the personal mail at her discretion, usually waiting until the end of the week to bring it all by, but this particular one I want right now. I'm not interested in waiting.

The light knocking at the door echoes in the small room, and I look at the clock. It's only three minutes later. *Not bad, Linda.*

"Come in," I call out and she does so quickly, closing the door behind her. She walks straight to my desk, not wasting any time. Her pink tweed skirt suit looks rather expensive. It's a Chanel, if I'm correct. I see she's putting that last bonus to good use.

"This is from today," she says, placing a compact stack in front of me, "and this-"

I stop her, waving my hand and pulling out the small, square, deep red envelope. "No need."

She collects the remaining mail, tapping it lightly on the desk to line everything up together and asks, "Anything else, sir?"

The use of sir catches me off guard, and for a moment I wonder if she knows who the sender of this particular piece of mail is, but her face is passive. And it isn't the first time she's called me sir. Most of my employees do. Linda just happens to use it less often than most.

I shake my head and say, "That's all." The lines around her eyes are soft, and her lips hold the faintest form of a smile. Linda's always smiling despite having to deal with me. She takes my hot temper in stride. That's one of the reasons I'm eager for her to stay.

She nods her head before turning on her heels. I wait until she's gone to open the envelope.

I watch her leave and listen to the door click shut, leaving me in my spacious office alone and in solitude. Just the way I prefer it.

I finally open the envelope with the letter opener on my desk, avoiding the black wax seal embossed with a bold X entirely.

The thick cream parchment slips out easily from the elegant envelope, and the handwritten message is in Madam Lynn's beautiful penmanship. If nothing else, I admire her flair.

I can practically hear her sultry voice whispering in my ear as I read the sophisticated script.

Dear Sir,

An auction is to be held and I personally wanted to invite you, Lucian. It's been far too long, and I know you're in need. Renew your membership first.

I'll see you soon,
L

An asymmetric smile plays on my lips as I take in her message. I may be a Sir, but she is certainly a Madam. I sit back in my leather desk chair and tap the parchment against the desk as I debate on whether or not I should attend.

It's been nearly a year since I've been to Club X. Even longer since I've had a Submissive, and only one of those was purchased at one of the monthly auctions. She lasted the longest, but only because she was required to.

It would be a nice distraction from the mundane. I muse, staring absently at the back wall lined with black and white sketches from an up-and-coming artist.

Before I can decide, my desk phone rings, bringing me back to the present. I lean forward with annoyance and answer it.

"Stone," I answer.

"Lucian," my sister's voice comes through the line. It's bright and cheery, everything my younger sister embodies.

Bubbly is what she likes to be called.

But her happiness doesn't rub off on me. Not after reading the fucking emails from our parents' lawyer. I doubt she knows, and it's not her fault.

She reminds me of them, though. I wish it wasn't like this. I wish I could separate the two, but I can't. They manipulate her, and it's only a matter of time before they'll come up in conversation. Shit, our parents could be why she's calling now.

"Anna, how are you?" I ask her casually. I trace my finger along the wax seal of the envelope as I listen.

"I've been good, but I've been missing you..." she trails off as her voice goes distant. I don't respond. I don't care to admit my feelings either way. Yes, there's a bit of pain from losing contact with my sister, but she chooses to keep in touch with them. She made that decision. And I refuse to have any contact with them.

"It's been too long," she says in a sad voice and then her tone picks up. "We should do lunch sometime soon."

I take in a long breath, not wanting to commit to anything. Lunches are quick unless it's a business meeting. Then they aren't really lunches. But beyond that, I don't have much to tell her. I'm certainly not going to be telling her what she wants to hear.

"Maybe soon," I finally reply.

She huffs over the phone, "You say that when you really mean no." Her voice is playful and forces a rough chuckle up my chest. She may only be nineteen, but Anna's a smart girl. I can't deny her. No matter how much I wish I could, I have a soft spot for her.

I lean forward and pull up my calendar. "I can do Thursday."

"Deal," she quickly agrees, and I can practically feel her smile through the phone. It warms my chest that I can make her happy. Unlike the rest of them, she doesn't take, take, take from me. She truly just wants to see me.

"I've missed you, too, Anna."

"Well you won't have to, since I'll text you and see you on Thursday," she says confidently.

"I will. I'll talk to you then." I'm quick to end the call before she can drag me into a longwinded conversation. She can do that on Thursday for all I care.

"Talk to you then. I love you," she says brightly.

"Talk to you then," I answer and hang up the phone.

As I do, my eyes catch sight of the card and I pick it up and rise from my desk, slinging my jacket over my arm and thinking about the last time I was there.

It's been a long time since I've set foot in Club X.

And a visit is long overdue.

CHAPTER 2

DAHLIA

G*od, I wish I could wear this color,* I think to myself as I slowly slide my fingertips over the rich, velvety purple fabric that lays across my desk. A fabric that will hopefully be turned into an award-winning gown. I suck in a breath, holding it and hoping that I'll be able to contribute to the design.

It's the new in vogue color this season, and it's only a matter of time before models will be flaunting it down the runway. I just hope that I can eventually be one of those fashion designers that proudly walks the runway at the end of a successful show. One day.

I like purple; it's probably up there with red and black as one of my favorite colors. I just don't look good wearing it. I gently lay the fabric down on the desk, thinking. Black suits me better, and it's probably why nearly all of my closet consists of black and greys. Even now, sporting dark silk slacks, a blouse the color of midnight and a cropped black leather jacket with my dark brown hair pulled up into a sleek ponytail, I look like I'm modeling for the grim reaper.

I think I need to stop wearing so much black, I tell myself, *maybe then I'll stop being so damn depressed.*

I take a deep breath and shake off the thought, taking the advice from my therapist to focus on the positives in my life. Black may be slimming, but it doesn't do the spirits any good. I just read a study on colors and the effects they have on the psyche and mood. I huff a small laugh. It was an odd thing to be tested on in my History of Fashion Development class, but it was eye opening.

Today has been wonderful, though. Actually, the past two weeks have been a dream come true. Growing up, I was heavily intrigued by fashion. Christian Dior, Gucci, Prada, Michael Kors, you name it. If it had a name, I wanted to wear it. I dreamed of cutting fabrics and sewing them into gorgeous gowns. One of my favorite gifts my mother ever got me was a drawing pad and a huge set of colored pencils for sketches. I filled the entire book up in only a month.

Over time, my obsession morphed into a lifelong dream of wanting to work in the fashion world, and up until several weeks ago, it looked like that fantasy would never come to fruition. But I finally got my foot in the door, and I'm not going to let this opportunity slip through my fingers.

Now I'm sitting here with my own office on the top floor of Explicit Designs, working one of the most coveted internships in town, living out my wish. It's unbelievable. Seriously, I absolutely love this job. I get to see all the latest designs and in-style fashions, meet quirky, interesting people and be involved in the entire creative process that goes into making these magnificent creations. It's funny how things turn out.

Especially considering how I'd almost given up.

A surge of anxiety twists my stomach, and I frown. It chills me to know how close I'd been to abandoning everything, how close I'd been to letting the darkness overwhelm me. Thinking about it makes me shudder, and I try my best to push the unwelcome thoughts away. It's a constant battle. Dark thoughts always seem to be waiting in the shadows of my mind--stalking me, haunting me, and then pouncing right when I think things are going good.

But things are better now, I try to convince myself. *And I need to focus on being happy.*

A clinking sound pulls me out of my reverie and causes me to look up. I see my boss, established fashion designer Debra Ferguson, through the glass window of my office, gathering her things and getting ready to pack up for the night.

This is the one thing I don't like about the floor I work on. The whole area is a large open space with floor-to-ceiling windows surrounding the offices, and there's virtually no privacy. Everybody can see everyone else. I suppose it isn't so bad, but I do miss my privacy.

I watch as Debra, who's clad in a fashionable red dress that hugs her matronly frame, slings her oversized Prada purse over her right shoulder and slides on her Gucci shades. For a woman in her late forties, she exudes the kind of sex appeal you would find in someone half her age, and it's one of the reasons why she's so popular. To me, she embodies everything I want to be when I'm her age: intelligent, confident, sexy and in complete control of her destiny.

As she makes her way out of her office, she doesn't bother looking my way. For a moment, I wonder if I should step out and tell her goodbye before she leaves. It would be the polite thing to do, yet I stay rooted in my seat.

I shouldn't, I tell myself, feeling a sense of self-consciousness wash over me. *I'll probably just annoy her.*

I don't know why I think that way. Debra has been mostly gracious to me. I suppose I'm intimidated by her. At least that's what I think it is. I'm new, and still trying to learn my place. There are only a dozen or so people working here, and everyone has their own routines. I need to learn mine.

Feeling conflicted, I watch as she walks out of the large room and disappears from view. I let out a slight sigh when she's gone. I don't know why I get like this, why I let my own self-doubts cause me to miss out. It's infuriating. And it's a wonder I've even landed this job with all the insecurities weighing me down.

After gently folding and putting away the purple cloth before making sure everything is in order, I grab my vintage Chanel purse and sling it over my shoulder. The purse is a hand-me-down from my good friend and coworker Carla. We shared a class two semesters ago, and I know it's only because of her that Debra even considered me for this position. I owe her so much already. *But wow, this purse.* I run my hand along the plush quilted leather, still in disbelief that it's mine.

I nearly died when she gave it to me, as I'd never owned anything so expensive before. Let alone *vintage Chanel.* For the longest time, I refused to use it, scared I would somehow lose it or someone would steal it... or worse, I'd get wine or lipstick on it. Instead, I let it collect dust in my closet. I only started using it after Carla scolded me and said to stop being so worried about it. In her mind, it was just a purse, and what was the point of having it if I was never going to use it?

I'm about to walk off when my phone dings. Quick to see who it is, I whip it out. *It's Mom,* I think anxiously. *She finally responded to my text.* Instead, I'm greeted by a message from my roommate Callie.

Calgurl182: *Gonna be studying hard for my exams. Please be quiet when you come in from work. Thx*

I grin at the message. When I need to get a paper done, I study hard, but Callie takes studying to a whole new level.

And with exams coming up, I know Callie's level of anxiety must be through the roof. I can totally relate to her not wanting to be disturbed.

After making a mental note to be quiet as a mouse when I enter our tiny apartment near campus, I flip over to my last text with my mom and my grin slowly fades.

Hey Mom, I know I told you about landing my dream job recently, but things are really tough right now financially. I've had to pay for so many things, a used car, clothing, rent, tuition... all these things have left me a little strapped and I'm not sure how I'm going to afford to pay for my next semester. I hate to ask, but can you help me out? I'll pay you back as soon as I get the chance.

Love you,

Dah

Staring at the blank space where her response should be, I feel dejected. I wasn't expecting much from her, but she could have at least responded and let me know that she cared, even if she can't help me out financially. I've had to pay for college myself. Which was fine when I had a job, but this internship doesn't pay anything, and I couldn't keep my retail job and also work here. I'm fucked. I was hoping my mother would be able to help me out. But this is the third text I've sent about money, and she hasn't responded to any of them. She sure as hell reminded me that she was going on vacation with her new boyfriend though.

It makes me feel like I'm low on her priorities. But maybe she just can't handle dealing with added stress right now.

She's been distant lately, and I know even before she started dating this current boyfriend she was having a really rough time. The last few years while I've been at school, my mother has grown apart from me. I can't help but wonder if it's because I remind her too much of my father. I hope not, because it'll only make me feel worse, maybe make me resent my father more, if that's even possible.

Just thinking about him sends a shiver of apprehension down my spine. I don't know if I'll ever forgive him for ripping our family apart. For letting what *happened* to me, happen. Even now, I still can't fathom it. My father was supposed to be my protector, my guardian. *He let him hurt me.* That fact shakes me to my very core, and occasionally, I suffer nightmares over it.

It's been better lately though. I swallow thickly and grab my coat.

Stop bringing this up. I've had a relatively good day, and I don't need to screw it up by living in the past. I'm never going to get over it if I keep wishing things had turned out differently. What I need to do is quit worrying and figure out a way to pay for my tuition next semester. I square my shoulders and nod my head at the thought, feeling my confidence come back. I'm going to make this work and have a life I'm proud of.

Just thinking about my money woes stresses me out. I can't help but think I'm going to be worn thin by having to work in order to pay the bills on top of doing this internship. That's not even factoring in the time I'll need to study for school.

I need to figure something out by next month. After finals, there's the holiday break and I can do something then. I'll find a way to keep this internship *and* pay for my classes.

Steeling my shoulders with resolve, I walk out of the office as I think to myself, *One way or another, I'm going to find a way to make some money on the side. Even if it kills me.*

CHAPTER 3

LUCIAN

My sister loves this part of the city, the hustle and bustle of Main Street with the crowds always walking by. I don't understand it. We could go anywhere, but she always asks to come to this particular cafe.

I take off my jacket and sit at a bistro table hidden in the shade, back in the corner. With my back to the stonewalled building, I can at least face the crowd.

We're still outside so she'll be happy, the crisp fall air rustling the newspaper in my hand. I place my forearm on the edge of the page and look out past the crowd while I watch the cars pass.

I grew up in the city. Only a few blocks from here actually. It doesn't make me like the city any more though. I huff a humorless laugh. Maybe that's why I don't care for this environment.

Too many reminders.

"Can I get you anything?" a waitress asks. Her sweet smile stays in place as she waits patiently with her hands clasped in front of her.

"Coffee black, with one sugar," I reply, and as I order I hear my sister's squeal and the loud clicks of her heels on the pavement.

She looks like she belongs here. Happy and dressed in the latest fashion, she fits right in with the people you'd expect to see in this part of town. She runs up to me and wraps her arms around my shoulders, making the waitress take a step back. She's the only person I let touch me. I just don't fucking like to be touched. But Anna can. She never hesitates to do what she feels like doing. I admire her for that.

She pulls back and takes me in; her cherry red lips make her brilliant smile look even whiter.

"Lucian," she says sweetly before turning to her left and finally taking notice of the waitress.

"Oh! Sorry!" she apologizes, her shoulders scrunching as she backs up and practically falls into her seat.

"No problem," the waitress says and laughs it off. "Can I get you anything else, sir?"

My eyes lift to the waitress. Ever since I got that invitation, it's been more and more apparent how many people call me sir.

I shake my head and give her a tight smile. She's a petite blonde, with a cute button nose and angelic face, but she's not my type. Not that it was on the table... but I'm sure it could be, if I wanted.

The waitress turns to Anna and before she can even ask, Anna orders while taking off her cream leather jacket, "Can I have a salted caramel latte with cream and four Splenda and an extra shot of espresso?"

She does not need that extra shot, but I keep my lips closed. I've learned not to give my sister advice, since she's going to do what she wants to do anyway. And me keeping my mouth shut makes her happy.

She sighs comfortably as the waitress leaves with a nod.

"How are you?" I ask her easily. She smiles brightly, pushing her hair over her shoulders and leaning forward.

"Everything is going so well." Her eyes soften as she says, "Thank you for paying my tuition." Her voice is subdued, but sweet. "It really means so much to me, Lucian. I know-"

I stop her. I know she's grateful, but she doesn't have to keep telling me. "Of course, I'm glad you're enjoying your classes."

I was honestly worried. My sister is naive, and I wasn't sure she'd enjoy college at all. She's never been much of a book person, or the studying type. But if she wants to go, I'm happy to help her so long as she takes it seriously.

She leans back, silencing her thanks and looks at the paper. "Are you in it today?" she asks. Her eyes are wide with curiosity.

I shake my head as I say, "No."

"Bummer," she says as she slumps back into her seat and I

chuckle at her expression. I'm never happy to be in the paper. I didn't start this business to be a public figure.

And up until the last few years, whenever I was in the paper, it wasn't good public relations. They say any publicity is good publicity, but they're dead fucking wrong.

The tabloids were not a fan of my playboy lifestyle. And neither were the stockholders. It didn't take long for me to change the business over to a privately owned company, but still, my company suffered because of my childish antics. I had to tone it down. No more fucking every pretty little thing who begged for my cock. I thought getting married would solve that problem--fuck, I thought I was in love.

I was a fucking fool, and I have the alimony checks to prove it.

If my name is never mentioned in the papers again, I'll die a happy man.

I started this company when I was Anna's age, back when I was only nineteen years old. It's odd to think that, considering how I still see my sister as young.

That was the year I split from my family. Realistically, I'd already been on bad terms with my brother. He's a jealous prick, and I have no intention of ever allowing him to be in my life again. Even back then, things were tense between us at best. At the time, I wasn't even speaking to him. But at least I still had my parents. Or at least I thought I did. Before I knew what it was like to be stabbed in the back.

I had to drop out of college. I huff a humorless laugh at the thought. My parents didn't try to help, and I simply couldn't afford it anymore, so I left.

A friend from one of my classes reached out and said he'd front the money for the business I was always talking about, and all he wanted in return was to be a silent partner. It was almost too good to be true. Zander's been at my side more times than not, even when my family decided to rip me apart and steal every penny from me that they could.

With Zander's startup capital, I built the company of my dreams from the ground up. He had the money, and I had the vision. It was perfect. And success came easily and exponentially.

My expression hardens, remembering how proud I was to give my parents a car. A brand new car. I forget what model, and it doesn't matter at this point. It wasn't good enough for them, and they wanted more. I couldn't though. I needed the cash flow for the business, it was growing so rapidly, and I could hardly maintain the expenses.

The day my bank account was drained and checks were bouncing was the day I cut those money-hungry assholes out of my life.

They stole thousands from me. I wasn't even going to sue them until they tried to do it again and then tried to sue *me*. I couldn't believe it. My own parents. We'd never been close, but they were still family. I don't understand it, even to this day. Had they given me time and believed in me, I would have been able to give them everything they ever wanted.

And I would have.

But that's not how it happened, because that's not how the world works.

Years have passed and time after time, I've learned it's better simply not to trust a damn soul. I have Zander and a few friends, and of course my sister. But no one else. It's better that way.

The waitress brings us our coffee and Anna's quick to bring hers to her lips, not caring that it's probably kissed-the-sun-scalding-fucking-hot.

She winces, putting the coffee down and bringing her fingers to her lips. I shake my head slightly, a grin slipping into place. I hide it by blowing on my coffee, my eyes on hers, but my amusement goes over her head and she takes another sip.

She'll never learn.

"So," my sister says as she starts trying to look me in the eye, "I'm going to have a holiday party." My spine stiffens, and the answer is on the tip of my tongue. She's been trying to include me in family events and work me back into our family. It's not happening. I was never close with any of them. I don't have a need for family. I don't need relationships in general. I'll do anything for my sister, but I'm not going anywhere near my parents.

She holds up her hands defensively and says, "They won't be there."

I'm taken aback and shocked; my brows draw in, and I consider what she's saying. "Did something happen?" I ask.

A sadness crosses her eyes quickly. But I see it there, and her lack of a response tells me that something did happen.

My voice is cold and hard, but not toward her, and she knows that. "What'd they do?"

"Nothing," she says softly, her shoulders folding inward. She looks down at the lattice table.

Usually I'd snap at whoever was sitting in front of me lying, saying nothing's wrong when there's obviously an issue, but I wait patiently for Anna to continue. She's hurt, and it's showing. I know she'll tell me what the deal is, but she just needs a moment. She traces the metal openwork design of the table absently. "They were just upset that I accepted your offer to pay for my classes," she tells me slowly, her eyes finally reaching mine as she visibly swallows.

My fists clench at my side, and my jaw tenses. Those fucking bastards. Why hurt her? All they care about are themselves.

"They just don't understand," she continues, picking up her coffee cup with both hands. She takes a hesitant sip and then says, "They just need a little time. You know how they..." she shrugs, "lash out."

My heart thuds in my chest as I calm my rage. *Hothead.* I used to be a hothead. But I'm wiser now, and she doesn't need my anger.

"Are you alright?" I finally ask.

She gives me a sad smile and says, "I am." Her hand reaches for mine on the table and I take it. "I promise I'm okay. But they won't be coming to the party."

She clears her throat, and I give her hand a quick squeeze before letting go. I knew they'd make her choose between me and them. Cowards.

"So..." she draws out the word, "are you coming?" I can hear the vulnerability in her voice, and it shreds me. I can't leave her with no family at her event. But a fucking holiday party?

"Please say you'll come," she implores.

I suck in a breath and concede. "I'll go." Five fucking minutes is all she'll need. Knowing her, she'll be busy socializing and won't even notice once I'm gone. I'll just make an appearance to make her happy.

She jumps in her seat and reaches across the small circular table, giving me a tight hug. It forces a smile to my lips, and I pat her back in return.

She finally sits and all seems right with her world again.

"You need a date," she says confidently. No doubt she already has some friend from school lined up who she thinks is perfect for me.

I don't trust a soul.

I don't put myself out there to be stabbed in the back and taken for granted.

Besides, the auction is coming up.

"I don't, Anna." I click the side button on my phone,

knowing it's about time to leave. And I'm right. "I do need to get back to work though."

She pouts and says, "But I just got here."

"You were late, Anna." I stand and slip my jacket back on, buttoning it while she leans over and kisses my cheek.

"Fine," she says, smiling. Her voice lowers as she says, "I'm really happy you're going, Lucian."

I give her a smile, feeling a slight pain in my chest. I'll go, but I'm leaving as soon as I fucking can.

"I'll talk to you soon."

I'm still tense as I walk away. My family, the memories... the fucking lawsuits. It's just another reason that I prefer to stick to my routines and stay away from all this shit. I don't need anyone in my life, and they sure as fuck don't need me in their lives.

CHAPTER 4

DAHLIA

"**I**s something bothering you?" Carla asks me intuitively before taking a bite out of her celery stick that's slathered with a generous smear of peanut butter.

We're having lunch on the third floor of the building in Explicit Designs' famed Divanista cafeteria. Although we share the building with other companies, this room is exclusively for our use, and it's one large open space with glass tables with shiny steel legs set up sporadically around the room. The floor-to-ceiling windows on the back wall provide a breathtaking view of the skyline downtown. Naturally, I've opted to sit right next to one of the windows. I love the landscape. It's one of the reasons I chose to come to the city here for school.

For my meal, I've decided on a diet soda and an apple. It's

not much, but considering my mood, I don't have much of an appetite. The stress of not having enough money is really getting to me. I wish I could look past it, but I can't. I don't see a way out of this mess while still keeping this internship. And backing out could ruin my career before it even gets started. It's a no-win situation, and every day it's becoming harder and harder to deny that I'm fucked.

I pause in mid-sip of my diet cherry cola, taken aback by the question. While I'm not in the best of moods, I think I've been doing a good job at appearing happy. I guess I've failed. But I'm trying to stay positive. I think if I hang in there, I'll figure something out. It's just easier said than done. "I just woke up feeling a little bit under the weather," I say. "Other than that, no worries." I give Carla my most reassuring smile and take another sip.

Carla's not fooled by my fraud, and she sets down her celery stick and gestures at me. "C'mon Dah, I know you better than that."

Crap. I want to tell her my problems, but at the same time I'm reluctant. I don't want her to think I'm hitting her up for money, especially after she gifted me that vintage purse. It would be embarrassing. I like Carla, and don't want to jeopardize our friendship by appearing desperate. "No," I say firmly. "Really. I'm fine."

Carla looks unconvinced. "You sure?"

I nod. "Mmmhmm."

Carla scowls, and then a second later growls, "Liar." She holds her glare, but when it appears that I won't be spilling the beans, she lets out a resigned sigh. "Alright, I'm not going to keep prying... for now. I'll let you get away with staying mum, but you're going to have to tell me what's bothering you sooner or later." Her celery stick whirls in the air before she takes a bite. The snapping sound makes me smile. If Carla's good for something, it's making me laugh.

After a moment her expression turns serious and she says, "Dah." There's a shift in tone in her voice, and I know this must be something important.

I swallow down my bite and answer guardedly, "Yes?"

Carla's fingers play with the edges of her celery stick. "I have a question."

By now she has my undivided attention, and worry laces through my chest. *I hope this isn't bad news. Or some sort of nasty gossip about me. I don't think I can handle any more stress.*

"Yeah?" I dare ask.

Carla hesitates a moment, as if unsure how she wants to proceed, and then she leans forward and says beneath her breath, "Are you into BDSM?"

I sit back in my seat, stunned. *Whoa. What the hell?* After a moment, I let out a nervous chuckle. "Where'd that come from?" My cheeks are flaming hot with a bright blush although Carla seems unaffected. She cocks a brow with a small smile, but doesn't answer right away.

"Carla?"

Hesitating, Carla licks her lips and studies me as if she's weighing whether she should tell me anything further. "I'm in a club," she says finally.

"What kind of club?" I ask cautiously.

"Promise you won't tell anyone," Carla demands. The lightheartedness I'm used to with her vanishes from the conversation entirely. "Or I can't tell you the rest." Her eyes flash with an intensity that is unnerving.

I don't know what Carla's getting at, but she has me on the edge of my seat. "I swear," I say. At this point, I'm dying to know what the hell this is all about.

Carla stares at me long and hard as if assessing my honesty before leaning forward slightly and whispering, "I'm in a BDSM club."

I stare, not comprehending. I know what BDSM is, but I'm just not clicking with what she's saying. "Do you mean some kind of cult?"

Carla freezes, and then lets out a small laugh. "Heavens no. Nothing like that." After a moment, the amusement fades from her face. "But it's not really something we talk about, though. No one is allowed in if they don't sign a non-disclosure agreement. Absolutely no one." Her last words are uttered in harsh tones, conveying the need for complete secrecy this mysterious club demands.

Wow. "Why in the world would anyone agree to that?" I

ask. My body heats some with the implications of what that could mean.

"Because of the clientele," Carla explains. "They're all powerful, rich and sometimes highly visible men. Men from all walks of life. Doctors, lawyers, businessmen, CEOs, celebrities... even congressmen and senators."

"You're kidding," I say, intensely fascinated, my breathing picking up.

Carla shakes her head and replies, "Nope." She sits back in her seat, taking a drink of her smoothie. "That's why NDAs are signed."

"So these men are married?" I ask after a moment of digesting this information. What she's saying is un-fucking-real, but I believe her. She's too serious to be lying, and now I'm just hungry for all the details.

Carla purses her lips thoughtfully. "I suspect some might be, but there is no way of knowing for sure." She puts the cap back on her smoothie and leans forward. "The club thrives on a secretive atmosphere, and though some of the Subs know the Doms' identities, they're forbidden," her hands fly outward, increasing the intensity of her words, "to reveal or share any knowledge of them outside the club." Her brows pinch together slightly as she continues, "I think a lot of men are just young, eligible bachelors that are looking for a place to sate their sexual appetites, so most Subs get to play with a free conscience."

Subs and Doms are all familiar terms to me... I mean,

everyone's read <u>Fifty Shades</u>, haven't they?

This is all so intriguing, and I find myself leaning in and lowering my voice. "So what happens if a Sub exposes a Dom outside of the club, or vice versa?" I have to ask.

Anger flashes in Carla's eyes. "Not only are they subject to legal action, but they get kicked out and banned for life." She emphasizes the next words, "But these are people you don't want to cross." Her face is deadly serious as she warns, "This club is fun and exciting and intoxicating, but you don't want to be enemies with these people. I mean it, Dah." The mood lightens up some as she readjusts in her seat and says, "So just keep it between us."

I let her words settle as I look out of the window. It's a bit frightening, but thrilling at the same time. I can see why such a rule is in place. The club thrives on secrecy, so divulging identities would be a big no-no if it wanted to stay in business. Also, keeping things confidential is probably a huge draw for the members. I'm sure it's a lot more fun and thrilling for both sides to know they're engaging in something so depraved that they have to hide it. The risk of getting caught only increases the thrill. The very thought sends a shiver of want down my spine.

My eyes are drawn to Carla as she takes another sip of her smoothie, her eyes fixed on me. "So why are you telling me this again?"

Carla's next words nearly knock me off my seat. "Because I want you to come and check it out."

I laugh with astonishment. "What?"

"My boyfriend, you know, Bruce? We're both members. It's how we met, actually."

My jaw literally drops. That is a total bombshell I wasn't expecting. "No way!" A blush grows on Carla's face. So she's a Submissive! I never would have thought that about her. Well, I would guess she's the Sub in their relationship... I have to stop my line of thinking right now before I get too carried away.

Carla nods. "He bought me in an auction."

What in the world? "An auction?" I breathe in wonder. Carla's boyfriend *bought* her? My eyes widen, and I'm not sure how to respond. *What in the actual fuck?*

"It's nothing like that," Carla says defensively. "Auctions are something by which Subs and Doms can take their experience to the next level, and these men pay dearly for the privilege to do so. As dark as it sounds, it's benign really if you look at it from the Sub's perspective." Her voice is much softer now, and I can tell she's practically pleading with me to understand. And I'm trying. I really am. "The Dom pays high dollar for a sex slave for a month, and the Sub gets to live out her fantasy of being dominated. Sometimes, they might even forge a relationship outside of the club's perimeters if they decide they like each other enough, like what happened with me and Bruce." She smiles sweetly and bites her lip for a moment before shrugging. "So you see, no harm, no foul. Everything is clean, consensual, and terms and conditions are outlined in the contracts. No one has to agree to accept any terms that they don't like. Rules *must* be followed, or else."

"That sounds scary as fuck," I blurt out. "To just get sold to someone."

Carla's shaking her head before I've even finished my thought. "There's so much paperwork, and all of your desires and fetishes are clearly marked. Everything is consensual, and the club is all about making sure everyone is safe. Seriously. It's all about living out your fantasies."

I squirm in my seat. My heart's racing at the very thought of being bought. I won't lie to myself. If I knew it was safe...

"That's why I'm telling you this," Carla says, though I'm barely listening, lost in my thoughts. "Because you can get paid... if you're into that sort of thing, that is. I think you'd enjoy it. I'm pretty sure you need a good hard fuck. Or two. And I know you need the money right now."

My ears perk up, and my heart stills in shock. Is it really that obvious? "How did you know-"

She shakes her head, dismissing my worries. "You're new here, and these clothes are expensive. You don't drive your car to work, though I know you have one. And when I gave you that purse, you acted as if I'd given you a five million dollar engagement ring with how scared you were of losing it." Carla shakes her head again. "I might look like an airhead, but I'm not." She reaches across the table and gently places her hand atop of mine. "I want to help you."

I want to help you strikes something in me. My eyes focus on the table, and I'm absorbed by my thoughts.

All of what she's said sounds exciting and erotic, and being dominated is something I crave more than anything else. But the reason for it is dark and twisted. Just thinking about it causes a horrific scene that used to be a constant in my night terrors to flash in front of my eyes. It's been years, and I thought I was over this. But I'm not.

I can never get over what he did to me.

"Please stop," I beg, my voice choked with pain as I struggle in vain. I hear my own voice pleading over and over in my head and it sends shivers down my spine. I close my eyes and try to ignore the memory. His heavy body on top of me. The smell of his foul breath as he told me to be quiet.

"I told you to be quiet, you little bitch!"

I clear my throat and breathe out deeply. I focus on remembering where I am today, and how it's in the past. But the sound of his voice won't go away. The memory flashes before my eyes. My body tenses remembering how I looked around for my father. How I screamed out for him to help me.

I tried to fight back, but it was useless. My heart beats rapidly at the memory, pumping cold blood through my veins. I wish I could forget.

"Dah?" Carla asks.

I jerk my hands out of hers, startled. My breathing is ragged, and anger tightens my chest.

"Is something wrong?" Carla is peering at me with concern, and I'm freaked out at how I so easily spaced in an instant.

I clear my throat and unclench my fists that I hadn't realized were balled up. That fucking bastard. He'd taken so much from me, and hadn't had to pay for it. When I told my father about what Uncle Tommy did, he just laughed, not believing his brother capable of such a horrible thing. He chose him over me, and he refused to take me to the hospital. "Yeah, sorry. I was just thinking about what you've told me and how interesting it all sounds," I lie. I've never told anyone other than my parents. I'm ashamed. I know I have no reason to be, but I am.

Carla looks unconvinced. "You sure?"

"Yeah." I wave away her concern and swallow the bitterness that forms in my throat. I've never forgiven my father for not believing me about what Uncle Tommy did to me. The incident caused so much friction in the family that my mom ended up divorcing him. *That* had been awful with all the screaming, arguing and accusations flying about. I liked to believe that my mom cared the most about what happened to me. After I saw how she focused on what assets she would get in the divorce instead of making sure Uncle Tommy paid for what he did, I began to feel like she'd just used me as an excuse to leave my father because she wasn't happy in her marriage. "Please continue."

Carla hesitates for a moment, studying me closely. She

doesn't buy it, but I can't let her know what happened to me. I don't want her to get spooked. I give her a nod, and then she finally continues. "So anyway, if someone does buy you, half of the final bid goes to the club. But when the minimum bid is five hundred thousand dollars, you won't find much to complain about as far as the fees go."

I gape with shock. Five hundred thousand dollars? It takes a long moment for that to even register. It's a good distraction from where my mind was going. I don't want to dwell on the past. I can't.

"That much money?" I ask with disbelief in my voice. "You've got to be kidding!" I can't believe they'd pay that much money.

Carla shakes her head. "I told you, these men are powerful and wealthy beyond your wildest dreams. For some of them, a million is like a dollar bill. But that's not even half of it. They pay a hundred grand a month already for their membership; these men are absolutely fucking loaded."

I'm too stunned to speak. Everything that I could ever want is right at my fingertips... if I could debase myself enough to become someone's sex slave for a month. It's an idea I should find shameful, an idea you'd think would repulse me to my very core even, but I find myself... craving it.

I need this.

Years after my traumatic experience, I'd grown up with the desire to be dominated. Which is ironic, because my uncle was never harsh or rough. He held me down, but then I gave up. The things I need to get off are highly specific.

At first these feelings brought me shame, but I couldn't help myself. I needed to be controlled by a powerful man to get off. There was simply no other way. This caused friction with some of my partners.   My first boyfriend couldn't understand why I wanted him to force himself on me, why I wanted to be choked and slapped around while being fucked mercilessly. He could never know how I'd been violated, and how the very act had perverted me in ways I didn't dare say to anyone. I didn't understand either. I felt sick after every sexual encounter with anyone. With the help of a therapist, I started to cope with everything, past and present. I need to be dominated, but I need to know it's for pleasure and know that I have control. That I can stop it at any time.

"Some Subs and Doms wear masks to protect their identities," Carla explains, cutting into my thoughts, "so you can even opt for a mask if it makes you feel more comfortable." She grins deviously. "It adds enormously to the spice and sizzle of a sexual encounter."

Unconsciously, I think about being dominated by a masked man, held down and fucked until my insides are raw. The uneasiness from my memories starts slipping away. This could be good for me. This could help me in a way I'd never considered. I'm broken. I know I am. No matter how many times my therapist says otherwise, I know I'm broken. I don't want to live like this, but I don't have a choice. And maybe this is just what I need. A Dominant who knows what he's doing, someone who can give me exactly what I need. I can picture it, and all the dark things that make my pussy clench and nipples harden play before my eyes.

"Dah?" Carla asks.

I snatch my hand away from my neck, which I hadn't realized I'd been clutching while I was engaged in my fantasy, and shake my head. "This club sounds so crazy."

Carla flashes a wide smile. "'Cause it is! Trust me, you're going to love it."

CHAPTER 5

LUCIAN

A small grin slips into place as I take in another look, making sure I'm prepared. When I built this house, I made sure to have this playroom made. Its sole purpose is pleasure. *My pleasure.* Whatever kink I want access to, it's here. The walls are painted a deep silver, and the wood furniture is all black. It's masculine with clean lines, but it's the details that matter.

Hooks line the ceiling; for the sex swing, for chains. For whatever the fuck I want. And they're scattered in various places. If I want my Submissive dangling from the ceiling with no support, I can make that happen. I can have her arms secured above her head while I'm fucking her from behind, and there's nowhere she can go, no place to hide, nothing to lean onto except for me.

My eyes linger on the Saint Andrew's Cross in the far corner. It's one of my favorite tools for punishment. My dick hardens in my pants just imagining a sweet Submissive secured to it, pleading for her forgiveness. *Yes.* I fucking need that. I need that right now. The sling stand and spanking bench are next to it, but I hardly ever use those. Although I know some Subs prefer them, and I'm always willing to compromise.

I run my hand down the leather-lined paddle and look at the other tools in the drawer. All of them are new. Never used, not even once. I got rid of the ones from my last Sub and bought new ones for this auction. Nipple clamps, plugs, paddles, whips, ropes, canes, cuffs, blindfolds, the works. Everything my Sub could possibly need.

I gently set the paddle back where it belongs and shut the drawer, feeling as though I'm prepared.

At first I wasn't sure I'd be ready to have another. I wasn't sure I even wanted one. But the more I pictured how the evening were to go, the more I decided I need to buy one at the auction.

If I'm going to do this, I'm going to do it right. And for me, that means absolute control. I want a contract in place, and I want the privacy of my own home. I know some of the other Doms, my close friends included, prefer the company of the club. They have their private rooms there, and they leave and go about their lives as though it's just a hobby. But for me this is so much more.

It becomes a borderline obsession once I've met the right woman. One who wants her needs filled, needs that complete my own.

I take a seat on the bed in the center of the room and pull out the mask from my pocket. I've worn a mask every time I've entered the club, like most of the high-powered men do. I learned the hard way that there are consequences to being open about this lifestyle. More than that, when I started my company, I realized very quickly how much my personal choices could impact the company.

Back then, when I was just getting started, I was a fool. I should have known better, but I was careless. I was angry about my family, and overwhelmed with women wanting to please me. It was more than flattering, and I was eager to enjoy their company. I was young and stupid. I shouldn't have been so reckless. It wasn't worth it, and if I could take it back, I would.

I quickly made a name for myself as a playboy in the tabloids. It was then that Zander introduced me to the club. It was a way to sate my desires, but still remain anonymous. My company no longer had to take a hit for my personal preferences, and it got the stockholders off my back. Not that they matter anymore. They can't do shit to me now.

Either way, it's best to be as private as possible. I have to avoid scandals and negative press at all costs. My livelihood is at stake, and women simply aren't worth it. The image of my wedding picture that used to hang in my living room flashes before my eyes. One failed marriage is all I need. She blindsided me and fooled me into thinking she felt something more for me. I should've taken a note from the Club X playbook and had her sign an NDA.

At least she took a paycheck to sign one after our hideous divorce. I don't know why I'm surprised. She just wanted a paycheck all along. Just like everyone else. They all just want a fucking paycheck.

I rise from the bed, feeling the need to take the paddle out again, but not having my Submissive at hand. I crack my neck and forget about the past. It's where it belongs. Tonight is about right now and needs that must be filled. I've put this off long enough. I *deserve* this.

I huff a laugh and smirk as I think about Zander's reaction to my text. He's the one who introduced me to this lifestyle. I learned to enjoy the release and the control gained as a Dominant. But it's more than that. It's the fulfillment of providing for a Submissive. Of training her and watching her become truly sated with pleasure. Earning her trust and devotion. It's a thrill, and a deeply satisfying one at that.

I've been craving it, but putting it off. It's difficult to put that faith in another person. The faith that they'll listen, and learn to trust you. It's even more difficult building trust that is real. But you can't hide your body language, or your primitive needs. My last Submissive tried to hide hers. I think she just wanted to play. But I don't do pretend and make-believe. I require perfection. I give this my all, and I expect every bit of the passion and energy that I put into this in return. But my last Sub didn't give me that. She was defiant and just wanted to be punished. Always. And each time she wanted it harder and more painful. I don't have a fetish for pain. That doesn't interest me. And she knew that. I took my collar off of her and never set foot in Club X again.

It's been almost a year since I've been to the club, a year since I've had a Submissive and given in to these baser needs. I'm more than ready to delve into my desires and put this room to good use.

I pocket the mask with a grin on my face. It's show time.

CHAPTER 6

DAHLIA

CLUB X

I suck in a sharp breath as I step through the club's doorway past the lobby and into a darkened ballroom that I can only describe as pure luxury. The floor is covered with plush, royal red carpet that is intertwined with breathtaking intricate designs, and the clicks of my heels are muted against the softness. The walls are painted a soft purple and are lined with gold trim, while golden sconces give off a red glow, suffusing the room with a sultry ambience.

High ceilings give the place depth as well as an airiness that makes my skin prickle with excitement. I touch the bracelet at my wrist. This one is temporary, but everyone is wearing them. It's just cream-colored rubber, but it'll look like Carla's when I join. *If* I join. The rubber is joined by three interlocking metal rings, with the center ring being black. She said it shows the other members that I'm a Submissive and that I prefer carte blanche, so the Dom has free range with me. The very thought makes my core heat with desire. Right now my bracelet is color is limited to cream because I'm learning. It will be apparent to everyone who sees it that I'm a BDSM virgin. There are other colors, but they aren't for my tastes. The knowledge makes my breath still in my lungs as men pass, glancing at my wrist with interest, but I'm still taking in the splendor of the club.

There are scores of finely set tables throughout the large room, as well as booths with velvet seating lining the walls. At the end of the room sits a stage, the large red curtains closed, hiding the secret of what lies beyond it. On the far left side, there's a high-end bar illuminated by neon blue light and outfitted with what looks like every drink known to man. Soft, elegant music plays over surround speakers that are artfully hidden, only adding to the luxurious vibe.

But the most exciting thing about Club X isn't the extravagant finery. It's the people. I walk behind Carla and Bruce, in awe of it all. My eyes dart this way and that, trying to take in everything, and I try, unsuccessfully, to calm my nerves. I settle my eyes on Carla's backside and my cheeks grow rosy as I admire the view. She looks fucking hot tonight.

She's wearing a short dress that barely covers her butt cheeks and hugs her body, showcasing every delicious curve. In fact, every woman here has on a dress that barely covers her ass.

They're everywhere.

Beautiful young women and masked young men that are dressed in slick high dollar suits fill the room. Even though their faces are hidden behind masks, I can almost feel the ambition, drive and authority radiating from these men, and it makes me weak in the knees.

Power. Wealth. Sex. It's all here, under one roof.

Looking around, I don't see a single man without a mask. Some are black and simple. Others are silver and themed with animals. The men sit at tables or booths alone, watching the room with an almost predatory gaze, while other men sit in groups talking amongst each other quietly. Other Dominants are accompanied by a beautiful girl or two, but it's clear who's in charge. Nearly all the women are in Submissive poses or in the act of being led around.

I watch as a tall man in a dark suit, his face hidden behind a metallic mask, walks past me holding a chain that clinks as he walks. It's attached to a dark-haired girl clothed in a silver shift dress. As she moves I can see the gown is nothing more than thin slits of fabric stitched together, her skin exposed in between the gaps. My eyes widen as the Dom tugs slightly, and the leash pulls at the collar around her throat. The Submissive tumbles forward slightly and the man catches her, pulling her into his hard chest and whispering into her ear. She smiles against his suit jacket as he chuckles and she nods her head slightly, looking up at him and responding with a soft, "Yes, sir," to whatever he's said.

He releases her and walks easily to a table where another man is already sitting.

The seated man, a tall blond, is eyeing the Dom's Sub with intense interest, his legs planted out wide. He mutters something to the Sub, and she blushes at whatever it is.

"Answer him," I hear the Dom command, looking at his Submissive with a heated gaze.

The Sub looks hesitant, although lust is easily read on her face before uttering something too low for me to hear and nodding slightly. At this, the Dom takes a seat at the table next to the blond man, and pulls his Sub into his lap, spreading her legs out wide and placing the balls of her bare feet on the leather-covered bench on either side of his thighs. The blond man moves in close and lowers the top of the Sub's dress, taking out her right breast. My lips part in disbelief. I watch as he takes her nipple into his mouth and as he slides his hand up between her legs. Her head falls back against her Dom's shoulder, and she moans softly with pleasure.

My breath hitches, and my eyes widen.

I glance around the room and then focus back on them. No one around seems to notice or think this out of the ordinary, and I feel my core heat at the erotic sight. Seeing as how this is a BDSM club, I expected to walk in on a wild orgy, where Doms would be fucking their Subs into submission, but the vibe is much more high class than that, giving off an almost secretive and seductive feel. But I'm still shocked to see something like that. My blood heats with desire, and my body feels aflame.

As I continue to watch the blond man suck on her tit, my nipples pebble and my breathing becomes ragged. I tear my eyes away, my cheeks burning with shame, when Carla whispers in my ear, "Sexy, isn't it?"

Carla is gazing at me, her breasts heaving as her eyes dart past me to the couple and then back to me. I can't get over Carla's dress; it looks expensive, and it's covered with glittering sequins. Both sides have long slits that show off her long legs, and nearly expose her pussy. Her hair is styled into a sultry deep side part, and her makeup is flawless. A Sub collar adorns her neck, and serves only to enhance her sexiness. It's a thin leather strap with a polished gold tag.

She leans in and whispers, her eyes still on the scene to our left, "Bruce doesn't share me. That's not our thing."

Her boyfriend and Dom, Bruce, looms behind her, his metallic mask glinting in the red ambient lighting, his dark, vested suit fitting right in with all the other wealthy men in attendance. He doesn't have a leash on Carla, and a lot of couples don't seem to have them either. Tonight, he let Carla be free of her chain, which she's told me she customarily wears, but has forbidden her to walk more than a few feet from him. I was there when he told her the rules, and I couldn't believe how eagerly she accepted them. She wants to please him. She craves his authority and his conditions. It's a dynamic that's foreign to me. I'd only met Bruce once before this. They seem like an average enough couple. But this is different. Much different. Here in Club X, he's the master of Carla's world.

Even though I know the basics of the dynamics behind a Dom and his Sub, it's going to take me awhile to get used to seeing Carla so subservient since she's such a hands-on, career-driven woman. I didn't expect this. It's one thing to fantasize about the lifestyle. It's quite another to be immersed in it.

But that's what being a Sub is all about, I tell myself, *surrendering all your control and power to another person and letting them take the reins.*

In that light, Carla is the perfect Sub.

I'm doing my best to fit in and copy Carla's behavior. I'm wearing a backless black dress that rises up to mid-thigh and the front side is cut low, showing off my ample cleavage. Salon-perfect hair, sultry makeup, spandex pantyhose and glossy nude pumps complete my look. I feel sexy, but at the same time I'm extremely nervous since this is my first time here. All the women present seem to be playing their roles flawlessly, and I'm unsure I'll be able to fit in. The thought brings my anxiety back to the forefront. I wish I could calm down, but I'm struggling to relax. Especially knowing the auction is tonight.

I can't believe I could be bought by someone. *Five hundred thousand dollars... or more.* The thought is surreal. I'm literally shaking in my heels.

"It's crazy," I breathe, making sure to keep my voice as low as possible and my eyes in a safe place. Carla warned me that even if I'm not claimed, I have to play the part of a Submissive. I can't do anything that would disrupt the fantasy the club provides. I don't want to offend anyone, and I don't want to get kicked out. Looking out among the sea of masked men, my heart pounds. These are men of power, men that could dominate me just like I want. An image of being held down by one of them flashes in front of my eyes. Before I realize it, I'm trembling with a mix of arousal and fear. "You were right about this place."

"Told you," Carla whispers so low that I can barely hear. She turns toward Bruce, looking for permission, and he gives her an imperceptible nod. "Come," she says quietly, gesturing at me to follow. "Let Bruce show you around before we grab a seat."

Without waiting for an answer, she begins following Bruce, leading me down a walkway on the right side. There's security detail as we leave the dining hall and go to the hallway where the rest of the club awaits. They check our bracelets and nod as we go through. Their presence only adds to the tension in the pit of my stomach. Bruce splays his hand on the small of Carla's back, and she looks up at him with obvious appreciation. My gait is awkward as several masked men turn their heads my way, their eyes boring into me. I feel self-conscious under their gaze, unsure about my place here. These are powerful men--doctors, CEOs, lawyers, senators, and I'm just some silly girl whose problems have led her here. But they don't need to know that. No one needs to know the reason I'm here.

I'm searching for a man of power to take control of me. To help me take control of my past. That's exactly what I need.

A dark feeling presses down on my chest as horrible images flash in front of my eyes. I do my best to push them away. I don't want to think about it. I came here to heal this darkness. This is going to help me. I know it will. I *need* this.

"How many of these men did you say work in government?" I whisper to Carla as Bruce leads us along, tearing my eyes away from those dangerous masked gazes and thinking of anything I can to ignore the stir of anxiety in my belly. Of all the men that Carla claims are members of the club, none seem more taboo than the ones holding public office. The risk of scandal is more substantial with these men, and I'm sure it makes the thrill of being with them all the greater.

"I'm not sure," Carla replies out of the side of her mouth, and I have to strain my ears to hear. "Just remember, the person that becomes your Dom could be anyone. A CEO, doctor, lawyer, governor, congressman, senator-"

"Even the president?" I interrupt. It's partly a joke, but the humor isn't evident in my voice. Mostly because of my nerves.

Carla pauses as if shocked, then shakes her head and chuckles softly. "No... at least..." a look of uncertainty comes over her face and she concludes, "I don't think so."

If the President of the United States is a member of Club X, I think to myself, *then this entire country is going straight to hell.*

I have no idea who's going to buy me. Every fucking time I signed a piece of paper to be included in the auction tonight, it nearly made me sick. I'm so anxious and worried. Anyone can buy me. At the same time, it's exhilarating. The only thing that keeps me from freaking the fuck out is knowing that all of my preferences, my hard and soft limits—meaning things I will not do and things I might try—are all in the contract. The contract itself was sixty pages long. Every possible detail and interaction between the buyer and submissive was included. And it must all be followed to the letter as to what my *preferences* are. The club is strict about filling out all the paperwork Madam Lynn emailed me. Plus, talking to her and Carla gives me faith that this is going to be the fantasy that I want and not some fucked up horror flick.

"Here's the Sex and Submission store," Carla says, gesturing as Bruce stops us in front of an opening into a large room along the wall. Inside, there are rows of shelves filled with all sorts of sex toys and BDSM devices. There are dildos, whips, chains, ropes, nipple clamps, elegant butt plugs and every kind of sexual toy you could imagine. I watch as several Doms walk around with their chained Subs, picking out their toys of choice to be used on them later. "Obviously, you'll be making stops here in the future. Just don't get too carried away." There's humor in her voice and I appreciate it, although I still feel muted in my excitement. My inexperience in this new environment is making me tense, and I feel overly self-conscious.

We continue on the tour and Bruce leads us upstairs through a long hallway filled with rooms on either side. Like the floor below, the hall is filled with opulence, with the same lush carpeting, beautiful painted walls, luxury furniture and upscale art pieces.

As we pass each room, I can faintly hear the sounds of smacking flesh and pleasured cries through the thick, fancy doors.

"Here are the private apartments," Bruce says as Carla stops, indicating a door off to the right. "This is where... well, you can pretty much guess what goes on. These are safe places for the Dom and his Sub and where they can get to know each other's limits in private."

There are men in dark suits lining the hallway, and they look like they mean business with their dark glasses and buzz cuts. It's obvious they're here to make sure no one violates the rules.

As we move through the hallway, I hear more sounds of debauchery that make my pussy clench on air; the crack of a whip followed by a soft cry, and then more noises of smacking flesh as if a man's low-hanging balls are smacking up against a wet pussy.

I want to be in there, I think to myself, my mind racing with base thoughts. *Being dominated.* My body tingles with anxiety and heated anticipation. I take in a staggered breath. Soon. I swallow thickly as my palms start to grow damp with perspiration. It's overwhelming.

We reach the end of the hallway and then Bruce leads us down the steps into another corridor that lets out into a large room filled with Doms and Subs who are in the act of role-playing and even having all-out sex.

"This is the playroom," Bruce says, nodding at the scene in front of us.

I hardly hear him. My eyes are on a Sub who's on her knees, being face fucked by a muscled, ripped, naked stud in a mask. He thrusts forward, forcing her to take all of his big cock to the ball sack, then he throws his head back, groaning with absolute pleasure.

Fuck, I say to myself as my pussy clenches repeatedly and my nipples stiffen like stone, *that's so fucking hot.*

That dark act of being forced is what turns me on. It's what I crave above all else. It used to shame me to my core, but now it's the only way I can get off.

My breathing comes out in pants as I watch, imagining being taken by force by someone like this masked man.

"We should go back now," Bruce informs me quietly,

turning to me. He watches me with a keen eye, taking in my flushed cheeks and heavy breathing, and an amused smile touches the corner of his lips. "I'm ready to eat."

I take deep, full breaths to calm my racing pulse and say nothing as Bruce leads us back to the dining room and to an empty table near the giant stage. As I take my seat, I notice several masked men's eyes on me, staring me down as if they know I'll be up for auction soon. My cheeks burn at their gazes, almost wishing one of them would come take me and relieve my throbbing pussy, but I ignore them. I know I'm not supposed to look at them unless they tell me to. Yet I feel that some of them sense the desire that burns in me, the need to be dominated. I wonder if it's attracting them, like a moth to a flame.

A wave of anxiety washes over me. What if it's one of these very men looking at me who buys me tonight? Will I be good enough for them? I'm sure that most of them are used to trained Submissives, but I'm new. I'll need to be taught, and I'll have to learn how to properly behave.

Total surrender is all I need, I tell myself. *The wants and needs of my Dom will be my wants and needs. His wishes are my command.*

I'm pulled out of my thoughts when a waitress dressed in a black uniform comes up with a gold-plated menu and sets it down in front of me and then looks at us expectantly. Bruce speaks first. "A dirty harry for my Carla," he says smoothly, "and a shot of whiskey for me." She nods, and turns to look at me.

"Just a water please," I say, swallowing thickly. My nerves are getting the best of me. My hands are shaking. Soon I'll be up for auction, and then I'll be owned by someone. A stranger. I should drink to calm down, but I need my wits.

Carla waves away my concern. "You're fine. You're going to love this."

That should soothe me, but it doesn't. She has no idea why I'm on edge. Well maybe she has an inkling about part of it, but she doesn't know the real reason that I want this. I can't shake my negative feelings. Even when we order our food and start eating, premium steak on a bed of wild rice pilaf, I feel anxious. I'm timid about how I'm going to go through with tonight. And actually, I'm fucking terrified. I'm new to all this, and as exciting and alluring as Club X seems, I'm not sure if I'm totally cut out to be a Sub, let alone being one for an entire month. I mean, what would happen, God forbid, if halfway through my contract, I decide that I can't take it anymore and want out?

But I can't, I tell myself. *More than the money, I need a Dom who's going to force me to face my fears. A Dom who's going to heal me, so I can move on with my life.* My blood cools, and I close my eyes. With everything in me, I know that I need this.

CHAPTER 7

LUCIAN

The door to my Audi R8 closes with a gentle click. It's rare that I drive myself anywhere anymore. I need the time to work, and with the heavy city traffic, having a driver frees up a good hour for work. It's even more rare that I have to self-park. Club X has a valet option, but no one uses it. The clientele here is well known, and members have our own gated parking on the side of the club. The lot is littered with expensive cars all rivaling the collection I have in my garage. Aston Martins and Porsches catch my eye in particular.

It's practically a treasure chest for men like myself.

I hit the lock, which echoes a small *beep* in the chill of the night, and stroll toward the entrance. My mask is already in place. It's simple, and made of smooth, black thin leather that wraps over my eyes and covers the bridge of my nose. Silk ties keep it in place. I actually purchased this one here. The club sells a wide variety of masks. They sell everything you could ever possibly dream of or need for this lifestyle.

As I step closer to the nine foot high carved maple doors, I smile wickedly in anticipation. Inside of this club is another world entirely.

It's a world of sin and darkness. A world of high-end luxury, an adult playground.

The darkness this time of night only makes the exterior of the club more alluring. The deep red up-lighting along the columns is barely a hint at what's waiting within. From the outside, you'd have no idea what you were walking into if you weren't already familiar with the club.

Even when the large doors open and reveal the interior, at first you may be deceived.

Before I can knock, the doors swing open silently. The staff is timed so well I don't even have to slow my pace. My shoes click on the stone entryway before being silenced by the plush carpeted floors. I walk in easily, feeling the warmth of the club in the foyer. The faint seductive music hums through my body, and a grin threatens to slip into place.

The air itself is provocative and mysterious. Nothing in this world exists like Club X.

"May I check your coat, sir?" the young woman asks at the long black front desk of the lobby on my right. Her voice is soft and even, and she holds my gaze steadily. Very little of her skin is shown other than the deep V cut in the blouse of her black pant jumpsuit. Her professional look is complete with natural makeup, and her blonde hair pulled back into a sleek ponytail.

She's wearing the same uniform that I recognize from all the years I've come here. It's easy to distinguish the employees in Club X. There's never a doubt that they're off limits and not interested in play. The professional touch that Madam Lynn requires is admirable.

Some things never change.

The air of familiarity makes my blood heat with the recognition of what's to come.

"No thank you," I state easily and walk through the lobby, the music increasing in intensity. The view of the restaurant calls to me.

Most guests are in awe of the dining area with its high ceilings and dim lighting. The stage takes precedence this late at night. The silhouettes of the go-go dancers are barely visible as the lights flutter around them in beat with the music.

There may be a doubt as to what Club X is if I'd come earlier and stayed for dinner, but when true night comes and the lights dim, the curtains open and the club comes alive. Sin around every corner, and a fantasy come to life.

I take a quick glance at the guests, and see a few familiar faces. I smirk, standing behind a round, tufted booth in the back of the room, the hallway behind me. Familiar faces aren't quite the right words, considering the men are all masked. But I recognize them, regardless. Senators, professors, CEOs... all men of power. My peers.

There may be secrecy in this building, but secrets are only as good as those who can keep them. Trust is something that doesn't come easily to me. But the contracts we all sign for our memberships are held sacred among us.

Judging by the simple clothing the women are wearing, there's no theme tonight. I suppose I should have known that. Madam Lynn likes to keep things simple on the night of the auction. One a month. No wonder the restaurant is only half full.

A couple passes behind me, and I turn to watch them walk through the hallway. His crisp, dark navy suit is at odds with the chiffon shift dress she's wearing that's practically see-through. Her pale pink nipples show through the fabric, as well as a hint of her pubic hair. She has a thin gold leash wrapped around her neck and held in his hand. It's a loose hold, and the chain is so thin I imagine it would easily break if she were to pull away from him. Without a collar on her neck, and judging by how quickly she's moving, it must be a punishment. She's to obey, or she'll no longer belong to him.

There are two men for security at the entrance to the hall. The restaurant is for anyone, but past this doorway is only for members. I already have the silver bracelet granting me entrance around my wrist, and I easily lift my sleeve to reveal it as I walk by. They nod their heads and remain still, their hands behind their backs.

Madam Lynn has stepped up her game in that department, they look like the fucking Secret Service.

The man picks up his pace and pulls a bit tighter on the petite woman's leash as they get closer to their destination. She lets out a small gasp and takes a few quick steps to catch up.

The Submissives in the club who are single and not claimed are able to roam, but there are rules. They must always display their submission so they don't break the fantasy the club provides; any action that disrupts scenes can lead to being banned or potentially punished if a Dom sees fit to take over the Sub and she agrees.

The Submissive's bare feet pad on the carpet as he leads her past the stairway to the dungeon and down a hall to the left where some the private rooms are.

They can be purchased for a decent price, all things considered. A few hundred grand a month is a reasonable rate. Each is numbered or named, depending on the owner's discretion; all are expansive, and fully furnished. They're tempting for the ease at which they can be used.

I've never had one. I do have a strong desire for privacy, but not here. I prefer the confines of my own home. It makes things difficult though, seeing as how the Submissive must agree to leave and to play where I'd rather be.

It's one thing to be consumed by the aura of the club, but

it's another thing entirely to unleash your desires in another person's care. And without the protection the club provides.

My steps pick up as I pass the divine pleasures of the club and make my way to the stairs so I can do what I came here for. The auction is starting soon.

Upstairs the atmosphere continues, but it's subdued. It's far more serious, and the music has vanished. In place of the dark red furniture and luxurious trimmings are simple round tables scattered with only two or three chairs around each. On the back wall is a stage, smaller than the one downstairs, with a podium off to the right. The deep red curtains are closed, leaving the room dark with little to occupy yourself with, but there's only one thing on every man's mind in this room at the moment.

"For you, sir," a man on my left says as I take in the room, my eyes adjusting to the darkness. I give the man a tight smile and accept the pamphlet he offers. My dick starts hardening, knowing my new Submissive's details are waiting for me inside. My body hums with desire, and my blood rushes in my ears.

"Lucian," I hear a deep voice call out in front of me. My eyes are drawn to a table near the back of the room and a small hand waving me to come to them.

A smirk slips into place as I pass Senator Williams. Although he's masked, I recognize the sharp features of his jaw, and the pale blue eyes peeking from the silver mask. I give him a nod, but he doesn't see. He's tapping the pamphlet on the table and staring at a man across the room. I don't recognize him, but I imagine it's someone on the senator's shit list judging by the look on his face. The knowledge makes my smirk widen into a grin.

"Interesting to find you here, Lucian," Isaac says in a smooth, lowered voice as I approach. The tables are separated enough for a bit of privacy. I unbutton my jacket and sit easily on the opposite side of Zander and Isaac. Two men I know well. Two men I trust.

"It's been a while," I say easily, taking in the sight of them. My eyes travel along Isaac's suit. It's light grey, and he's even wearing a striped silver tie. I'm not used to the look on him. The men in here are expected to be dressed in black tie attire, but it's been nearly a year since I've been back, and seeing Isaac in a suit is something that's more or less a rarity. Even though it's custom tailored, he looks like he doesn't belong in it. His rugged demeanor and casual stance offset the clean lines and hard edges the suit is meant to enhance.

He's simply not a man to wear a suit. If it were up to him, I imagine he'd be in jeans. Although I'm sure he's found ways to use the tie around his neck to his advantage. He's a contractor for private security, and you'd think he'd be used to dressing up. But he looks like he's itching to get out of his suit. Although I know the silver watch on his wrist costs a fortune. I suppose we all desire a bit of luxury, it's just a matter of personal taste in choosing how to go about it.

I glance around the room, the memories of the club coming back to me, but I stop when I see a man I recognize. It's not because I've seen him here before. Joe Levi. He has a mask on, but his sharp features are distinct, and his mannerisms are the same. He's a crook; a mobster, a villain. This room and club are filled with men of power and wealth, but a membership isn't something that can simply be purchased. There's a background check and a training course that must be completed first. Madam Lynn is out to protect the women here just as much as she aims to profit, but seeing Joe makes me question that.

I gesture slightly toward him, catching Isaac's eye.

"He's been here about three months now," he answers, and his voice is low.

"Are his tastes what I've heard them to be?" I ask soft enough that our conversation can't be heard by anyone else. Zander can hear, but he lets Isaac answer.

"He only comes to the auctions."

I nod in response and look back over to him.

"He's yet to buy anyone." Isaac's words settle in me as I take in the other buyers. Some I know, some I don't. The only one I'd rather not have in this room is Joe. But that's not my call.

"Are you suddenly in the buying mood?" Zander asks me. He's a man who fucking belongs in that suit. He was practically raised in it. Zander's from wealth; he oozes high class, and his neat black bow tie is the cherry on top. As a wall street mogul and heir to a sizable fortune, the designer look and gold cufflinks fit him well. With sharp cheekbones and piercing green eyes, his classically handsome look makes him fit in with this exclusive crowd. Isaac belongs here as well, but his suit is caging in a beast who wants out. That's the difference between them.

"I need a distraction," I finally answer.

"It's good to see you back on the horse," Isaac says with a smirk.

I huff a small grunt of a laugh. "I've just been busy."

Zander smiles at my response and looks as though he's contemplating opening his smart mouth for a response, but he doesn't. Instead he rests his elbows on the table and looks to the stage.

"Have you two already picked out who you'll be bidding on?" I ask. Although I've seen them at events and at a poker night here and there, no one's spoken about Club X or any Submissives or partners recently.

Isaac shrugs, moving his eyes from the stage to me as he answers, "I'm here more for the company. Just biding my time until the show tonight."

"Anything interesting?" I ask.

He raises his eyebrow and his blue eyes sparkle with mischief as he says, "Fire play."

"Ah," I answer and choose not to expand on my thoughts. I have no interest in fire play or anything that could cause serious scarring. No whips, no fire, no spikes or knives. My brow furrows, and I sit a little more comfortably in my seat.

"Don't get your panties in a twist there, Lucian," Isaac says with a grin that shows off his white teeth.

"Fuck off," I say easily.

The guys laugh, and I feel a little more at ease.

"Seriously," Zander says, "it's good to see you here."

I give him a simple nod. It is nice to be back. I can feel the adrenaline scorching my blood, and it's intoxicating.

I haven't been back since before Tricia. My ex-wife. I took her here a few times for some shows to see how things were performed. I let her pick out her favorites. The memory turns the corners of my lips down, and the excitement dims. But I shake it off, clearing my throat and ridding my mind of all thoughts of her.

I flip through the pamphlet, leaning back in my chair and scanning the verbiage I've read a time or two before.

There are strict guidelines that must be adhered to by both buyer/seller to gain entry and to continue membership.

Membership is one hundred thousand per month and allows members to attend auctions and enjoy all the privileges of membership.

All parties are clean and agreeing to sexual activities and must provide proof of birth control.

The women are displayed and purchased in an auction setting with a starting bid of five hundred thousand.

Subsequent bids will be in increments of one hundred thousand dollars.

NDAs are required, and paperwork will be signed after the purchase.

Any hard limits are noted at auction and will be written in the individual contracts.

The rose color of the Submissive indicates her preferences, so please take note.

Pink - Virgin

Cream - Finding limits/BDSM virgin

Yellow - Simple bondage D/s

Black - Carte blanche

Red - Pain is preferred S/M

No flower - 24/7 power exchange

The buyers must adhere to all rules of the club, or they will be banned and prosecuted. Submissives must also obey all rules, or buyers can take legal action and no money will be paid.

With the accepted terms and conditions, the willing participants of this auction are as follows:

As I turn the page to read about the women and their desires, the lights darken and a loud click prefaces the thick red velvet curtains opening slightly and the auctioneer walking onto the stage.

The auction is starting.

CHAPTER 8

DAHLIA

*J*ust *relax and everything will be fine,* I tell myself as I step into a room backstage to prepare for the auction.

There's a group of scantily-clad girls already getting ready, and some of them are naked, looking through a rack of skimpy outfits to find which one suits them best. None of them appear to be nervous like I am, or at least they're very good at hiding it.

If they can be cool and collected under pressure, so can I.

I suck in a deep breath, my palms moist with perspiration, my heart racing, and try to calm my nerves. I have to get a hold of myself. I don't want to walk out on stage and wind up fainting because I've worked myself up into a tizzy. I can do this. I just have to keep telling myself how much I need this experience.

Trying to ignore my anxiety, I make my way over to an unattended clothing rack near the rear of the room. I begin sifting through outfits, looking for one that best matches my personality. After a moment of searching, I let out a huff of frustration. I don't see anything that I think looks better than what I already have on. But I have to find something. And quick. The auction is only minutes away.

Just try on something. Anything. I'm sure it will look okay.

I'm about to snatch a red dress off the rack when the sound of clicking heels causes me to turn around. A gorgeous older woman walks toward me with a confidence that reminds me of my boss Debra; a woman in charge of her destiny. Her blonde hair is styled elegantly, her makeup flawlessly dramatic, and her voluptuous figure puts some of these younger women in the room to shame. She struts toward me as if she owns the place, her scarlet red dress clinging to her impressive curves with each step.

Madam Lynn. It has to be.

She stops in front of me, her face brightening into a friendly smile, and extends her hand. "Miss Days, what a pleasure it is to meet you." She shakes her head as if in wonder. "The picture in the email you sent doesn't do you justice. You are far, far more beautiful in person." She speaks with a polish that sounds very professional, something you wouldn't expect from a woman who profits from sex and submission for a living.

My cheeks become rosy at her compliment. "Thank you, Madam Lynn," I say, taking her hand and shaking it. Her hands are soft and warm like her personality. I'm surprised that this woman seems so down-to-earth, considering the awesome wealth that makes up her club. I originally pictured a snobby woman with her nose stuck so far up in the air that she wouldn't know what down was, even if she fell flat on her face.

Madam Lynn flashes me another warm smile filled with straight, sparkling white teeth. "You are very much welcome."

I finger my newbie Sub bracelet nervously, wondering why she's here to greet me personally. Had I done something wrong, like unknowingly violated a rule while on my tour with Bruce and Carla? It would be just my luck.

Seeing my worried expression, Madam Lynn waves away my concern. "You're fine, dear. This is simply protocol. I check on all my girls before every auction to make sure everything's running smoothly, and no one is having second thoughts." She pauses and peers at me with concern. "You aren't having those... are you?"

Of course I am. But I'm not telling you that. "No, I'm good," I blurt out almost immediately. I cringe at how fraudulent I sound and wait for a response.

Madam Lynn simply smiles, placing a gentle hand on my shoulder. "Good to hear. I think you're going to make a fabulous Submissive, and will make a very lucky Dom super happy."

Her words fill me with a confidence that I haven't felt all

night, and I'm grateful for her encouragement. "Thank you, Madam Lynn," I say respectfully.

Madam Lynn nods. "Mmmhmm." She begins to turn away, but then stops. "Miss Days?"

"Yes?"

She points to a skimpy gold sheer number on the tail end of the rack. "Might I suggest that one for you? I think it will look good on you, and serve to enhance your beauty. It fits your personality perfectly. I'd stick around to see you try it on, but I need to go check on the other ladies before time runs out." She winks at me in parting. "Good luck at the auction."

I watch as she glides off and begins talking to other women in the room before my eyes fall on the dress she picked for me. It looks okay enough, but I won't see what it really is like until I try it on. I take it off the rack and examine it. Gold and sparkly. There are large gaps in the material, and it's more revealing than what I have on. Blushing, I undress behind the rack, hiding from the other women, and then slip into it, enjoying the feel of the soft material against my skin. I walk over to a large mirror and then suck in a sharp breath when I see myself. The gold material sparkles against the light, enhancing my figure and tanned skin in ways I didn't think possible, making me look utterly gorgeous.

Madam Lynn was right. This looks perfect on me. It's flattering in all the right ways. It's sheer, but the metallic color hides my body well, compared to the other women in the room. I look around at them all crowding around the vanities and chatting away. It's almost like what I'd imagine a strip club could be. Or a burlesque show. My heart pounds harder in my chest, and I pace my breathing as I calm myself down.

I'll have to remember to thank her after the auction. And also ask if I can keep this dress.

"Please check over the pamphlet one more time and make sure everything is accurate," a heavyset woman with greying hair pulled into a bun says behind me, startling me.

I've read this pamphlet over and over. The sheer amount of paperwork I've had to fill out and read is exhausting. My stomach churns as I remember the psychological section. There was a box for me to write in. I was supposed to disclose my problem. I didn't. I suck in a sharp breath as a lump grows in my throat.

I reach out and take the pamphlet, trying to catch my breath. I need to get a hold of myself. I open it up and read through the small description of me, and the list of kinks and fetishes I'm willing to try.

As I look through the rest of the pamphlet, I begin to feel like a prostitute. I try to push the thought from my mind as I take a seat at one of the chairs lining the wall , but I can't shake the feeling that I'm selling out. Cheapening myself. Just because there's a written contract involved, how is this any different than selling myself for sex?

I can end up being a rich guy's perverted fuck toy and nothing more and hating myself after the contract is over.

The thought makes me sick. It's because of my money troubles that I'm thinking like this. And I have to be honest with myself--the money is tempting, and would solve so many problems in my life so easily. I want to cry for thinking about myself that way. But that's not what this is for me. This is much more than just some easy money. And if this turns out to be anything less than what I want for myself, I'll walk away from it all. The money doesn't matter. I need more from this. I need the fantasy. My body heats, and my pussy pulses with need.

I can't back out now. I have to go through with this. Carla's gone through this same process, and look how happy she is with Bruce. She's a successful career woman by day, and a perfect Submissive by night. Looking at her, you would never guess she's leading a double life. Using her as an example, I really should have nothing to worry about. I have to believe that this will help heal me, even if the man who buys me doesn't know about my problems. He gets off on his sexual fantasies, I get the money and continue with the therapy that will help me. It's mutually beneficial for the both of us. A win-win.

Feeling slightly better, I close the pamphlet. And not a moment too soon. The large woman who handed me the pamphlet is suddenly herding all the women in the room together.

"It's time, ladies," she announces. "Good luck with the

auction tonight."

As I line up with the other women, it's obvious that the rest of them have done this before and they all know each other well. I pull at the hem of my dress as the women in charge call out names. I'm the second name called, and I force my legs to move as I walk to the front of the line. I peek out as she opens the door, but the curtains are closed. The floor of the stage is a shiny dark wood, and the walls are covered with a thick wallpaper with a subtle cream paisley pattern. Other than the gorgeous wallpaper, the stage is empty. There's no detail whatsoever. It lacks the details and luxury that the rest of the club has in every other room.

I suppose the only detail on the stage will be each woman as she takes her turn in the auction.

"You seem very nervous," a woman behind me says. The blonde woman in front of me turns around, and the two women look at me, waiting for me to respond.

"A little," I breathe. No shit I am. Who wouldn't be?

"Relax, you'll make good money, and it's so much fucking fun."

The woman in front of me lets out a small laugh and then smooths her red dress. The dress itself is provocative. The deep V in front dips so low that it nearly shows her belly button, and there's no back at all to the halter dress. It's so revealing, but it suits her well. "It's always a good time, and all the times I've been in the auction, I've never seen a woman not have a man bid on her."

The woman behind me nods her head and leans forward to peek at the empty stage. "I already know who's going to be bidding on me this time."

"Your boyfriend?" I ask.   The women laugh, and my insecurity is almost unbearable.

"I don't have a boyfriend, and I'm not interested in one," she answers with confidence.

The woman in front of me looks at me as though she's wondering why I'd even mention a relationship. I feel fucking sick to my stomach, but I close my eyes and remember this is just sex. Good sex. Sex that's going to give me what I need. When I open my eyes again, I see the woman in front of me smiling.

"That's what you should be focusing on," she says with a knowing look. "Just enjoy yourself," she concludes as her eyes roam my body and she looks out beyond the door to the stage once more.

Madam Lynn opens the entrance door behind us with a clipboard in her hand, and a petite brunette in bright pink high heels in tow. She looks like she's struggling to keep up with Madam Lynn's confident stride toward the front.

"Alright, ladies," Madam Lynn doesn't look up from the board as she walks toward the stage with everyone turning to face her. "We'll have Madeline first," she announces, then looks up and lets a playful smile grace her lips. "I wonder who you'll be going home to tonight?" she asks beneath her breath with a raised eyebrow. I didn't even think about leaving the club. I look around the room again and notice all the duffel bags. There are only a few. But it looks like some women have packed an overnight bag. Shit. For the first time since I've seen her, the beautiful woman in front of me actually blushes. "Dahlia, you'll be next," she says as she turns to me, and I can feel everyone's eyes on me.

Madam Lynn's eyes travel down my body and then back up to meet mine as she brushes the hair out of my face. "Let's keep your hair behind you and not cover up your breasts. Take your bra off as well." She moves on, continuing to list the ladies and doing a thorough check of each as my heart sputters in my chest. Another assistant is carrying a handful of roses, ten total, in a variety of colors. She passes each girl a rose in turn. I carefully take the cream-colored rose as she hands it to me. Although the thorns are gone, I still feel as though simply holding the rose in my hand is going to hurt me.

I step out of line and reach behind my back to unclip the bra and let it fall. My breasts are perky, but they sag slightly from their weight. I look in the mirror, feeling even more self-conscious.

"You're beautiful, Dahlia." I turn to face the woman behind me. "These men know what real women look like."

I clear my throat, taking my spot back in line and trying not to hide myself, fiddling with the soft petals of the rose. "Thank you," I say as confidently as I can.

The urge to cross my arms is strong, but I fight it.

"Madeline," Madam Lynn calls out her name as she opens the door wide. "Let's go, my dear."

Madeline walks confidently out onto the stage and I walk quickly to take her place behind the door. Madam Lynn's hand is firm on Madeline's shoulder as they walk, their heels clicking and Madam Lynn whispering in Madeline's ear. She finally releases her, lining her up in the center of the stage.

It's so bright. Spotlights are shining on her body, and their intensity makes the dress pointless. You can see everything. Fuck. The breath is stolen from my lungs as I look down at my own dress and hear a microphone being turned on.

"Welcome, gentlemen, it's time for the auction." At Madam Lynn's words, the curtains slowly open and Madeline straightens her shoulders, standing tall for all the men to see.

Sucking in a deep breath, I prepare for the auction to start.

CHAPTER 9

LUCIAN

"How about her?" Zander asks with a raised brow. Neither him nor Isaac have their bidding paddles in hand. Judging from their conversation, they aren't interested in the women tonight. There are at least fifty men in this room, and the pamphlet lists only ten women tonight. So I'm perfectly fine with them sitting this one out. I'd like to find someone who'd suit me well, and there's one I'm eager to see.

I shake my head as a man I don't recognize starts the bidding off at five hundred thousand, raising his white paddle that's barely visible.

The woman is beautiful, and the pamphlet indicates she's experienced as does the black rose in her hands. But the next woman is the one I'm impatient to see.

"Six hundred thousand," the auctioneer says loudly, searching through the crowd and then nodding his head. "Seven to the gentleman on the right." I turn and see Zander's raised his paddle.

He smiles broadly as the original man yells out, "Eight hundred thousand!"

"Stop fucking with him, Zander." Zander's grin doesn't fade as he sets the paddle down and shrugs at Isaac.

"You better not do that shit to me," I tell him. Cocky bastard.

"Is that what you do here?" I ask beneath my breath.

Isaac shakes his head and watches the stage as the woman is sold for nine hundred thousand dollars. "He just started doing it out of sheer boredom. One day you're going to win one of them," he turns to face Zander, "and then what?" he asks.

"Then I'll have myself a Submissive," Zander says flippantly. Isaac answers with something, but I don't catch it.

The woman I've been waiting for walks out on stage. Her nude heels click on the ground, and it's all I can hear as she walks in what seems like slow motion. Everything else turns to white noise, and the only sound in my ears is the steady *click, click, click* of her nervous steps.

She's utterly gorgeous, but there's an obvious innocence about her. I thought I'd be interested when I looked at her information initially, but now I'm certain that I have to have her.

Treasure. She's the one. Her gold dress clings to her figure and sparkles beautifully, as though she truly belongs in it. The gold tones only make her sun-kissed skin that much more beautiful. My dick is already hard at the thought of my hand leaving a bright red flush across her lush ass.

She centers herself on the stage, looking nervously at the auctioneer and then behind her, at Madam Lynn.

The dusting of sparkles on her dress barely hides her soft curves. I want to see all of her. I want to feel her soft skin. I grip the paddle tighter and rise it up high. "Five hundred thousand," I call out, starting the bid before the auctioneer can ramble like he did with the first woman.

A man in the far corner, features behind a grey mask that covers three-quarters of his face raises his paddle. "Six."

Another man in the far back who I recognize as Stephen White, heir and owner of a few local car dealerships, raises his paddle. "Seven hundred thousand."

Although the thin wood of the paddle pierces deeper into the sweaty palm of my hand as anger washes through me, I maintain my calm demeanor and raise my paddle again. "Eight hundred thousand."

I watch Dahlia, my treasure, as her skin colors a beautiful red on her chest and up her cheeks with a blush. My dick twitches at the thought of seeing that color on her ass. I can imagine how she'd squirm in my lap as I smacked my hand down with a blistering beating. Gripping her tempting ass before spanking her over and over.

"Nine. One million," the auctioneer points at each man

as they raise their paddles, upping the cost. I don't care how much I have to pay. She's going to be mine. "One million one hundred thousand. One point one."

There's a pause, and he looks around the room through his spectacles. "One point two," he says as I raise the paddle.

"One point three," he calls out as the last bidder, White, raises his paddle again. I turn to face him, and although he must be able to feel my eyes boring into the side of his face, he ignores me.

I raise my paddle once more and keep it in the air this time. "One million four hundred thousand," the auctioneer says. I watch as White raises his and then takes a peek at me as the auctioneer rattles off, "One point five," my paddle still in the air.

"One point six," the auctioneer says, pointing to me and then looking back to White.

"Shit's getting real," I hear Zander say out of the side of his mouth. His humor doesn't do anything to ease the anger flowing through me. She's mine.

White finally breaks my gaze and sets his paddle on the table. I stare him down as the auctioneer says, "One point six million, going once... going twice," he takes a final look around the room and I swear to God if anyone were to speak I'd lose my shit, "Sold! For one point six million."

I watch as the woman, Dahlia, gasps. My treasure is ushered off the stage with unsteady steps in her patent leather heels as she tries to collect herself. A smile grows along my lips as I stand to go to the office in the back where I'll collect her after the auction is done.

"Congratulations, sir," Zander says with a smirk.

"You should have bid two mil, you pussy," Isaac says to Zander, and I finally huff out a small laugh.

"Maybe next month I'll fuck with him," Zander says before taking a sip of his whiskey.

I ignore them and watch as Dahlia disappears from my sight.

I knew the moment I saw her that I had to have her.

And now she's mine. I *own* her. A few sheets of paper stand in the way. And then tomorrow morning, I'll have my Submissive all to myself. I'm dying to get a taste tonight, but the rules must be followed. And that means one last night to herself, and then she's mine.

The door to the office I've been sitting at for nearly an hour finally opens, and my hand tightens around the tumbler on the table. The ice clinks as I move the cool glass, bringing it to my lips. My eyes never leave the door as I take a sip of the aged whiskey.

It opens seamlessly, revealing Madam Lynn in her scarlet dress. She's a gorgeous woman with poise and grace, but I ignore her entirely, waiting for Dahlia to be revealed. Her shoulders are hunched inward slightly, and her head's down. Although she originally walked in with her eyes on me, they immediately fell to the floor.

It's like she's scared to look at me.   Maybe she's overwhelmed. I imagine that's normal, and I'll be sure to put her at ease. The pamphlet only gave a tiny bit of information about Dahlia, my treasure.

I know she's a first-time Submissive.   Her information indicated she hasn't been trained, which only makes my dick harder and me more eager to get her back home and in the playroom. So her looking down is an instinctual Submissive behavior. That's fucking perfect.

She looks even more beautiful close up as she walks to the glass table and takes a seat across from me and next to Madam Lynn. The madam slaps a stack of papers down on the table, finally gaining my attention.

She smirks when I look at her.

I only care about two sheets in that entire packet.   The non-disclosure agreement, and the page where Dahlia signs and consents to be my Submissive for the next thirty days.

"Madam Lynn, Dahlia," I greet them both, although my eyes are firmly on Dahlia. At the mention of her name those beautiful wide eyes look up at me.

"Are you going to be keeping your mask on?   Or is it acceptable to reveal your identity?" Madam Lynn asks.

Ah, yes. I slip off the mask and place it on the table. I'd

forgotten about the damn thing. I know Dahlia has already signed an NDA for the auction, and I want her to get a good look at me and read my expression.

I don't want her to question how much I truly want her.

"Dahlia, meet your new Dominant, Lucian." Madam Lynn leans back in her chair as Dahlia extends her hand to me.

A smirk plays at my lips. She's so fucking cute. I play along, shaking her hand. When our skin touches, her soft small hand in mine, my body ignites with desire. The urge to pull her close to me takes over, a spark heating between us. I release her and move my hand to my lap before I do something stupid and take her before the contracts are signed.

I clear my throat. "Let's get this over with."

"Eager, are we?" Madam Lynn thinks she's funny.

She sets a sheet of paper in the middle of the table and points to a list with a thin silver pen. The list has several boxes checked, but some are empty.

"Do the two of you consent and agree upon the following conditions?" I look through the list carefully. The checked boxes are the ones that Dahlia desires, and the unchecked boxes are hard limits, meaning we won't be engaging in those activities.

I read through each stipulation carefully, making sure our tastes are agreeable. For the most part, it's my choice on things while she's still finding her limits. She's new to this lifestyle, so she's been assigned cream as her color for now. With over fifty specific fetishes on the list there are only a handful of hard limits, such as: scat, blood, breathing and permanent marks which remain unchecked. I agree with her on all of those, and I'm not interested in them either.

The boxes checked include the usual: anal, bondage light and bondage heavy, nipple play, deprivation, spreader bars, and other kinks and fetishes. Fisting is also included, which makes me look up at this petite little thing with mild surprise. She blushes violently as I take in her expression. We could work up to that. I imagine she checked it as a soft limit.

I sit back and nod my head, accepting the pen from Madam Lynn. "Everything looks perfect to me." I sign on the line.

"Wonderful," Madam Lynn says as she takes the sheet and pulls out another. I'm getting anxious, and I can't stop staring at my treasure. She's not looking at me, and I know she's nervous; in fact, I enjoy that she's nervous. But I'm going to need some privacy to take full advantage of that.

We sign a few more papers, including the NDA I require.

"Alright, and now to summarize the above terms and conditions. You, Mr. Lucian Stone, are agreeing to act as Dahlia Days' Dominant at the locations of your choice for the duration of the next thirty days which will end at precisely one minute past midnight on the fifteenth of the following month of December. As her Dominant, you agree to the terms and conditions in the above contract, including and accepting that at any point Miss Days can terminate the contract and end the relationship entirely."

I nod my head as Madam Lynn pauses and glances at me. "And Dahlia Days acknowledges and accepts that by leaving this arrangement, all monetary gains in the sum of half of one point six million, which is the equivalent of eight hundred thousand dollars." Dahlia looks as though she's going to faint as Madam Lynn rattles off the figure, "will be forfeit." She turns to Dahlia, who's completely lost in thought; it's obvious she's still in slight shock. After a few seconds, my treasure sits upright and nods her head.

"Yes, I understand."

"I'll need you to sign here," Madam Lynn says, and I wait for Dahlia to sign, my hands itching for the pen. "And Mr. Stone," Madam Lynn hands me the pen and I'm quick to scribble my signature.

"Your thirty days starts tomorrow," Madam Lynn says, finalizing the procedure. It's about fucking time.

"I'd like you at my address at eight in the morning," I say and scratch my address down on the pad of paper. I took tomorrow off just so I could enjoy her fully for the first day. I may be a workaholic, but my treasure is a real treat, and I'm going to need time to explore every inch of her body and test how every subtle touch affects her.

"But I-"

I stop and look up at her, not knowing why Dahlia would object. Maybe she doesn't have transportation. "I can have a car pick you up, if you'd rather?" I offer her.

"I can drive. I just wasn't expecting it to start so early. And I thought maybe we'd be at the club?"

"You'll be in my playroom for training, and you'll be available when I want you, which will be all times of the day and night, treasure." She gasps slightly, and her eyes widen.

"I-" she starts to answer, and then looks at Madam Lynn as if she's the one she should be speaking to. *I'm* her Dom, for fuck's sake.

"You what? Tell me what's bothering you." I'm getting irritated by her hesitation, and my tone reflects that. She doesn't seem too bothered by it though, which is good. She's going to have to get used to it.

"I have an internship," she answers hesitantly. The poor girl hardly looks like she's breathing. She can't even look me in the eyes. Her shyness, nerves and even the hint of fear are all endearing.

"Why was that not included in the contract?" I ask her.

Madam Lynn opens a folder and produces a sheet, sliding it across the table. I glance at it, and her schedule is listed as flexible.

"I didn't know my schedule ahead of time," she explains meekly.

"Do you know it now?" I ask her.

"For this week," she answers me quickly. I nod and let out a heavy sigh. That'll have to work.

"I'll need your schedule," I say and hold out my hand for

her to pass it to me from the pile of papers in front of her. She should have brought it.

She looks at the stack on the table and then up to me. Her eyes are gorgeous, a beautiful mix of greens and blue with a touch of golden brown. They're the most stunning hazel eyes I've ever seen. Her chest rises with a sharp breath as she says, "I-" she stops, and swallows thickly. "I didn't know to bring it."

My expression hardens, and I move my hand back to my lap. My fingers grip my thigh to keep from grabbing her ass and pulling her across my lap. She's unprepared. My dick is hard as a fucking rock knowing I should punish her. But I have to remember, she's new and still needs to learn.

"I can get it to you tonight," she says in a slightly more firm voice.

"Is that acceptable?" Madam Lynn asks me from Dahlia's right. I can feel her eyes on me, but I don't take mine off my treasure. I can't punish her just yet. But I'm going to give her a taste of it tomorrow. Whenever I'm able to get my hands on her.

"How many hours a week is your internship?" I'm already pissed that I can't have her whenever I damn well feel like it.

"It's forty hours," she says softly. Her quick reply with an answer I was expecting makes me relax somewhat. I can handle forty hours of her away. It will be good for her to maintain a social life. I swallow down my selfish desire to have her on call at all times. For now, this will have to do.

"What time are you done?" I ask.

"Around six," she says, then holds my gaze and nods.

Around six. I give myself a moment to calm down. She isn't trained. She doesn't know me. But she will, and she has so much to learn. "Precision and timeliness are important to me."

She opens and closes her mouth, clearly at a loss for words and then nods her head. That's a very good start. I'm enjoying this already.

"I'll need to know when and where to pick you up." I could have my driver wait there, or I could wait outside of wherever it is that she works as well, but I don't have any desire to wait around. I have a list of shit that needs to get done, and I want to know a specific time. More importantly, I want to hold her to this time.

"No later than six fifteen," she says confidently. *Good girl.* It's irritating as fuck that I'll have to wait, but I'll have her to myself tomorrow night. I'll bury myself in work until then.

"I'll need the address and your schedule sent to this number." I jot my number down and slide it across the glass-topped table to her. She reaches for it, but I keep my fingers on the paper and wait for her to look at me. "I expect that message tonight."

"Yes..." I can practically hear the "s" on the tip of her tongue. She looks up at me and then back to Madam Lynn.

"Ask me, Dahlia," I tell her. "If you have a question, I'm the one you need to ask. No one else."

"Sir?" she asks with those sweet hazel eyes peering up at me, filled with vulnerability. "Do I call you sir?"

My dick is harder than it's ever been in my entire fucking life. "Yes, treasure. You will call me sir."

She starts to ask another question, but then pauses for a moment and licks her lips. "Always?" she asks.

I shake my head gently. "In this club and when we're playing, but if I take you out, then no, I don't want you to call me sir." She nods her head, accepting what I've told her as I let my own words settle. *Take her out.* When would I fucking do that?

"Any last questions for either party?" Madam Lynn asks. She looks between the two of us, but her eyes linger on Dahlia. She's seen many of these auctions; I'm sure she's made up in her mind what type of match this will be already.

Dahlia shakes her head as she says, "No." Her breathing is coming in shorter and heavier, and I know the reality is setting in.

"No, I'm more than ready for tomorrow to begin. And make sure you pack a bag with your essentials and a change of clothes. You'll be staying the night."

Dahlia nods her head as she says, "I understand, sir." Her voice is small and her words barely more than a whisper.

"I'll see you tomorrow at six fifteen," I tell her as I stand and fasten the middle button of my jacket and then slip my mask into place.

"Yes, sir." Those sweet words stay with me for the rest of the night. The soft sounds of her submission from those plump lips are all I can think about. Tomorrow. Six fifteen can't get here fast enough.

CHAPTER 10

DAHLIA

"Lucian," I announce to Carla. "Lucian Stone. That's who bought me."

I'm leaning against a clothes rack, standing in the fashion workroom on the third floor early the next morning, organizing Debra's designs for an upcoming fashion show. I really want my coffee, but I'm so anxious I'm scared to drink any more caffeine in fear it will make me a jittery mess. I'm still in disbelief over the amount of money Lucian paid for me. *1.6 million.* Jesus. It doesn't seem real.

But it won't be 1.6 million after Club X takes its cut, and after taxes. In the end, I'll probably end up with less than five hundred thousand. Still a fuckton though. And it'll go a long way in getting a head start in life. I'm definitely not complaining.

I turn to look at Carla, wanting to read her facial expression for any kind of reaction, but she has her back turned to me.

She's putting the edgy outfits in their respective categories with ease, but I can hardly stay on my feet. I'm so exhausted. I was up all night, tossing and turning, consumed with thoughts of Lucian and reliving the events of the auction in my head. All I could think about was how gorgeous he was, with his dirty blond hair, chiseled jawline and that brooding, yet intense expression that made me feel like I was burning up inside while on stage and back in Madam Lynn's office.

Being up close to him had been even more intense. He radiated such power and a sort of mystery that made me hungry to know more about him. Even the way he spoke, with a deep growling voice throbbing with authority, filled me with sexual desire and made me want to fall to my knees and please him right then and there.

I remember the title he made me call him.

Sir.

A shiver goes down my spine as I think about the way he looked at me. Like he owned me. Like I was his property. I want him. Now. More than that, I crave his lips on mine, his touch on my body. I crave his... domination. I can picture him now, thrusting his chiseled hips against my ass, pushing every inch of his big fat cock inside of me as he wraps his powerful hands around my neck and makes me beg for more. The raw image flashing in front of my eyes makes my nipples harden, my core heat with desire, and my body tremble with anticipation.

I can't wait for our first meeting.

Six fifteen, I tell myself, sucking in a deep breath and pushing away the naughty images. *I just have to make it until then. Then I'll be all his.*

Carla slips a glittery red halter top on a rack, the clinking of the hanger snapping me back to the present, and then turns to face me, her face twisting into a puzzled expression. "Lucian Stone," she murmurs, tapping her index finger against her lips thoughtfully. It's weird to see her dressed conservatively today, in a black pantsuit and hair pulled into a ponytail, a far cry from the slutty outfit she had on last night. I'm struck once again by her ability to live this double life. Looking at her, you would never guess that she was into being someone's Submissive for pleasure. "Hmm," she says, closing her eyes, and repeating his name over and over to jog her memory.

Her eyes pop open a moment later and she frowns at me, causing my throat to drop into my stomach. "I'm sorry, Dah," she admits, shaking her head regretfully. "But I've never heard of this guy."

My mouth falls open in shock, my heart pounding in my chest. I don't know why it matters that Carla doesn't know Lucian, but I'm really fucking nervous. Going into the contract, I knew I'd be handing myself over to a total stranger, but I would've been more comforted by the fact if it were someone Carla knew and could vouch for.

"What?" I ask incredulously. "I thought you knew a lot of these men's identities." Maybe I feel anxious because I don't know what to expect from Lucian. He has an air of mystery about him that seems... intoxicating, but dangerous at the same time. Carla knowing something about him, *anything*, would help me feel more at ease.

She shakes her head. "I never said that, Dah. I just said that I know who *some* of them are. But I'm sorry if you got the wrong idea. I wish I could tell you more about this guy, but I can't." She pauses, lost in thought, and then shakes her head. "I wouldn't worry too much. This guy sounds like he *really* wanted you. It's been awhile since a chick commanded that kind of price." She scowls. "I'm jealous."

Before I can reply, Debra struts into the room holding a stack of papers in her hand. Once again, I'm reminded of how Debra resembles Madam Lynn--not in looks, but personality. She looks gorgeous today in black spiked stilettos, tight white pants and a silk black top that showcases her impressive chest. Her hair is done up into an effortless updo with wisps of hair framing her mature face and her makeup is vibrant, taking a few years off. But the most alluring thing she's wearing, as always, is her confidence.

"Good morning, ladies," she greets us with a smile,

walking over to a table on the side of the room and placing the papers on it.

"Good morning," we both reply in near unison.

Debra turns to face us and chuckles, shaking her head. "Ah. You girls are so cute! It makes me sad that I've brought more work to put on your plate."

Cute? If you only knew the depravity we're involved in.

I hold in a groan and hope it's not something too involved. I can barely keep my eyes open.

"What's that?" Carla asks curiously.

Debra points at the pile of papers. "I need you two to match the models in those folders with their respective gowns for my upcoming show."

"That should be easy," Carla says easily, and I hear the relief in her voice. "We'll get that done for you no problem, boss."

"Speak for yourself," I mutter under my breath, low enough that Debra doesn't hear. Carla grins at me. She knows I've barely gotten any sleep, but she's cheery anyway. Probably from the hard fuck she got from Bruce last night. My cheeks heat at the memory of Club X once again. I can't stop thinking about last night.

Debra shoots her a thumbs up. "That's the spirit. I knew I could count on you two." She starts to leave the room, but pauses in the doorway to add, "Oh, and by the way, I also need you two to come up with theme ideas for the after party. Usually Kevin comes through for me, but he's down with a nasty cold and I don't know if I can depend on him." She pauses to look between us both. "Can I count on you two girls?"

Carla nods and says, "Yes," but at the same time, I say respectfully, "Yes, Madam Lynn."

Debra must not have heard me, because with a flash of a grin, she's gone.

Carla turns to me, her expression shocked. "You did not just call her Madam Lynn!"

Placing a hand over my mouth, I let out a deep yawn that I can't control. "Sorry. I'm really tired." The cups of coffee I've drunk this morning have done little to wake me up, but something tells me that when six fifteen gets here I'll be wide fucking awake.

"Their mannerisms do favor each other though," Carla says thoughtfully, walking over and grabbing a stack of Debra's papers. "But you need to be careful that you don't slip up like that in the future. Madam Lynn's name is an open secret and who knows what clientele she has... even in this building."

It takes a moment for the implications of what Carla is saying to hit me. "Debra?" I ask incredulously, my jaw dropping open, "a Submissive?" Never in a million years would I think Debra would have a submissive bone in her entire body. She's just... too powerful for that.

Carla makes a face. "I'm not saying that she is. I'm just saying, would you have thought I was a Submissive without me revealing it to you?"

I shake my head.

"Okay then. Just remember the NDA you signed." She motions me over to an empty table to the side of the clothing rack. "Come help me sort through this mess right quick and then let's get lunch."

We spend the next half hour categorizing fashion designs and matching model profiles to the outfits they'll be wearing for Debra's upcoming fashion show. Carla is making quick work of the task, but I'm finding it hard to do even the simplest thing, tired and my mind filled with anxiety. When I screw up and pin a model's profile on the wrong outfit, Carla places a hand atop mine, her expression concerned.

"What's on your mind, Dah?" she asks.

Do you even have to ask?

"I just wish there was a way that we could find out more about..." I say, my voice trailing off. I don't know why I'm bothering. Carla has already said she doesn't know anything about Lucian. She can't conjure information about him out of thin air just because I want her to. I'm probably just worrying myself to death over nothing.

Carla shakes her head, her eyes filled with sympathy. She must think my worry is getting tiresome, but I can't help it. This is my first time doing something like this, and no matter how hard I try to relax, I remain on edge. "I don't think so, the club's rules..." her voice trails off as her face crinkles into a thoughtful expression. "I know!" she says suddenly, her face brightening, snapping her fingers. "We can look him up on the net!"

Oh my God, I'm so stupid. That's actually a genius idea. Why the hell didn't I think of that? I've spent all this time worrying when a simple Google search could have turned up dirt... if there is any.

Probably because all I've been thinking about is being fucked by him, I think to myself. "Let's cyberstalk him," Carla says, slinging a black slinky dress over the rack and throwing the model profile she's holding down on a table.

Uneasiness touches my chest.

"You're not going to be able to work unless you find out more about Lucian to put your mind at ease. So let's get it over with. You only have a few hours before you meet up with him, and you don't want to go into your first encounter terrified, trust me." She begins making her way over to the nearest desk, and I hastily slip the white dress I'm holding onto a hanger and place it on the rack. "What about all this?" I gesture.

"It'll still be here when we're done. C'mon. It'll only take a few minutes."

"You think Debra will care that we're doing this on a company computer?"

Carla practically rolls her eyes as she says, "Girl, you don't even wanna know what I've searched on company time."

Fuck it. My need to find out more about Lucian overrides

my caution of breaking the rules. "Let's do it."

She grabs a chair and slides it across the floor to sit next to me as I tap on the space bar to bring the screen to life. I take control of the mouse, and within a few clicks, pull up the Chrome browser.

The blank Google search bar sits in front of me, the cursor blinking.

"You ready?" Carla whispers, placing a comforting hand on my thigh and gently rubbing it.

I'm ready for anything that says this man isn't a sociopath, I think to myself.

Gulping, I nod, and my fingers fly across the keys. *Lucian Stone.* I stare at his name in the search bar, anxiety filling me. *What will this search reveal?* I wonder. Hopefully nothing. Back in front of Madam Lynn, he definitely didn't look like a bad man with his dashing good looks, but my opinion on that will change quickly if I find something I don't like.

"Dah?" Carla presses.

Screw it. Taking a deep breath, I tap the left mouse button.

The first few results that pop up on the screen are pictures of him, all of them incredibly handsome, and him with other young businessmen in suits. Some are even shirtless pictures of him on the beach, his incredible eight-pack abs proudly on display. Desire stirs in my stomach as I look at them. He's so gorgeous and built like a Greek god. Seriously, he looks like such a tall glass of champagne. It doesn't seem possible that

I'm now going to be his property for an entire month.

All that is going to be mine later, I tell myself. *Holy fucking shit.*

"Jesus," Carla breathes, her eyes widening at all the eye candy of Lucian. "He's fucking hot!"

"You're telling me," I whisper, clicking through several sexy pictures of him on the beach, my pussy clenching at the thought of having this man all to myself.

After admiring a score of pictures of Lucian, I scroll down the page and my eyes settle on a bold headline.

Man becomes youngest CEO to make eight figures.

I click on the article and begin reading. Carla is as well, and I can hear the faint wispy sounds of her lips moving as she follows along. It's one of her quirks, but it's slightly distracting as I read about how he dropped out of college and started his own company. It wasn't long before he rose to the top of the corporate world and made a name for himself.

The article continues listing Lucian's accomplishments, which I find quite impressive. There's nothing in the list that gives me cause for concern. My anxiety ebbing a little, I move on from the article and skim through the next few search results. All of them are about the same thing, talking about how impressive Lucian's rise to power is and how he's the next big thing in the corporate world.

Holy fuck, he's accomplished so much.

Insecurity stirs in the pit of my stomach, replacing the dread. Next to him, I feel like a complete underachiever. It's going to be hard not to focus on his status when I'm with him. I can only hope that he makes me forget who he is when we have our sessions, otherwise they won't be pleasant.

I scroll through a few more of the same types of articles spanning the last few years and take deep breaths, my anxiety ebbing slowly.

Satisfied there's nothing else to see, I'm about to close out the search page, when I notice another eye-catching headline that makes my heart jump in my chest.

Young CEO headed for tumultuous divorce.

Married for less than a year, CEO and sole proprietor of Stone Enterprises, Lucian Stone is headed for a vicious split with Tricia Stone, formerly Morgan. The couple has filed for divorce, citing irreconcilable differences although there are several rumors of an affair. And not what you'd expect. It appears Mrs. Stone has fled their home and is staying with an unknown "former friend." Tricia has been quoted as saying, "The last few months of our marriage have been difficult, and I simply can't continue in this manner. This marriage and divorce have certainly harmed my image, and I have no doubt that it will affect me for the rest of my life. This isn't what I thought we were committed to when we exchanged vows, and I am deeply heartbroken by the turn of events." Mr. Stone has failed to comment.

I close out the page, feeling slightly uncomfortable and wincing with a twinge of guilt. I shouldn't have dug past his company's history, let alone gotten into his personal history. Shit.

"Feel better now?" Carla is looking at me with relief in her eyes. I wish I felt the same. It seems she's just as happy as I am that nothing dastardly has shown up on Lucian. I probably would've driven her crazy had I not done this. "You found out that he wasn't a serial killer... and I found out that I missed out by getting stuck with Bruce."

"Carla!" I protest.

Carla gives me a playful smirk. "Just joking. But seriously, you okay now?"

No, I'm not. But I'm going to suck it up and deal with this until tonight. I nod my head. "You're right. I didn't find out anything that makes me want to back out of my contract, thank God."

Carla smiles with relief. "Good."

The rest of my day is much more productive, and I'm even able to come up with a kick ass costume theme for Debra's after party; Subs and Doms. Carla thinks it's an absolute hoot. She's just worried about how Debra is going to take it.

By the time six rolls around, the exhaustion I was experiencing earlier is gone. Like I predicted earlier, I'm wide awake and I can't stop trembling with excitement.

"I'm going to go freshen up and then wait downstairs for my ride," I announce to Carla, my hands trembling with nervousness and excitement as I stick the last profile on an outfit. There's still one last pile of clothes that needs to be organized, and there are sticker papers all over the floor. I'm supposed to help Carla clean it up, but if I do, I'll be late and I'm afraid of angering Lucian before our first meeting.

I can almost picture the anger in his eyes, and it sends a shiver down my spine.

Carla finishes hanging up a white ball gown, and then turns to grin at me. "Just remember to relax and enjoy yourself," she advises. "A good Dom will make you feel safe in surrendering to him." She pauses and bites her lower lip, as if unsure if she should say something else. "And let me know all the dirty details tomorrow!" she blurts out.

"Seriously?" I give her a pointed look. "But you just scolded me earlier about the NDA."

Carla scowls at me with consternation. "Fuck the NDA! Lucian is hot as fuck. I want to know what happens, or else!" She gestures at the leftover work. "Besides, you owe me for leaving me to deal with all this alone. Hopefully Lucian leaves a red print on that ass for me in revenge." She gives me a devious grin, and I imagine her mind is filled with dirty, depraved thoughts.

I blush furiously and let out a laugh. "My, my, that attitude isn't very submissive, is it? But okay. I'll be sure to take notes."

Carla mimics the thumbs up Debra loves to give when someone is doing a good job. "Good girl."

I laugh again and leave Carla to clean up our mess and make my way downstairs, my heels clicking against the floor. I walk into one of the work restrooms and make sure it's empty before I walk over to the mirror. I need to freshen up before I meet with Lucian's driver. I feel like I can barely breathe as I lean against the granite counter. I would've preferred to go home to take a shower after spending all day on my feet, but Lucian had been adamant. He wanted me right at six fifteen, and not a moment after. I shouldn't be surprised. This is a man who is used to getting what he wants. *And he wants me.* Again, I can hardly believe this is real. One point six million, with a super handsome and ultra-wealthy Dom willing to fulfill my fantasies. And eight hundred thousand of that money goes to me. It's just too much to take in.

Anxiety and desire roll through me thinking about the way Lucian demanded that I be available for him. Sitting there in that chair, he looked like a man that was dying of thirst. Like he would've done anything in that moment to get a drink of me. And I want to satisfy that thirst. My blood chills at the thought of him looking at me like my last ex did. Like somehow he'll know I'm not enjoying it. That I'll be disappointing him if I can't get off *when* he wants, *how* he wants. I take in a steadying breath. *No*, I think and shake my head. Neither of my exes would've even known about my problems if I hadn't told them. And this is about me pleasing Lucian. I can do this, and Lucian doesn't need to know about how broken I am.

After several deep breaths, I feel a bit calmer. I finish washing up, and focus on fixing my hair and makeup. When I'm satisfied with my appearance, I leave the bathroom and make my way out into the vast lobby and toward the front exit, marked by two glass double doors.

My heart seems to pound harder with each step, and by the time I reach the doors, I'm out of breath. I can't stop trembling. I'm filled with anxiety over what's to be my first sexual encounter in years. It's been a long time since I've been with a man, and the last few encounters only left me feeling disappointed and let down. A part of me is afraid this will end up being no different.

Outside, a Rolls Royce with tinted windows is waiting for me by the sidewalk. The driver is leaning against the car and immediately pushes off and straightens his shoulders when he sees me. I don't even have to guess whose car it is.

I place my hand on the cool silver handles of the glass double doors, steadying myself, my legs feeling like they're going to buckle. Another few minutes and I'll be running late. I need to get out there, but I have the sudden urge to run away.

I can do this. Everything is going to be okay.

Taking a deep, calming breath, I swing open the doors and walk outside.

CHAPTER 11

LUCIAN

I loosen my tie as I finally get to my penthouse. She should be here any minute. I wanted to be in the car with Joseph when he picked her up, but work took priority. Besides, we can discuss matters in the playroom. Quickly.

I'm ready to feel that tight pussy milking my cock. I couldn't even sleep last night I was so fucking hard for her. The last hours of work nearly killed me. I sigh heavily and toss my tie onto the large circular table in the front hall. Now that I'm home, she'll be able to relieve my stress.

Just knowing that simple fact makes every muscle in my body relax. As if on cue, I hear Joseph's footsteps and her heels walking down the hall.

I don't wait for him to enter. I shrug off my jacket,

leaving it on the front table with my tie and open the door myself. Joseph's walking behind Miss Days as he looks up and answers, "Ah, here he is now. Mr. Stone," he greets me.

Dahlia's stopped and looks back at me with widened eyes, staring at me with a mix of fear and lust. *Perfect.*

Joseph brings in the duffel bag he's carrying and sets it down in the foyer. He's a quiet man. He doesn't ask unnecessary questions, and that's why I like him.

"Thank you Mr. Brennan, that's all for today."

"Good day," he says then nods his head and turns to leave. I'm not usually so short with him. But right now I have one thing on my mind.

"Mr.... sir," Dahlia corrects herself and blinks several times, still not sure what to say or what name to use. An asymmetric smirk forms on my face. She looks gorgeous. Her hair is styled into loose waves and resting over her shoulders, covering her breasts. Her blouse is baggy, and hides her figure. It's fashionable, but it needs to come off. It would look far better on the floor than on my treasure.

"Come in, Dahlia," I say barely above a murmur, stepping back and opening the door wider.

She nods, and noticeably swallows. I wait patiently as she walks in slowly. I know she's timid, but that's going to change quickly. I'm going to enjoy the transition.

I stop her, with my hand on her waist and lean out slightly to show her the keypad on the outside of the door. "You'll come here every day, and Mr. Brennan will get you up the stairs," she turns and stares down the hallway to the elevator, "and here you'll enter in a code specifically for you so you can wait for me." I've already set in her code. "It'll only be active from six thirty to seven, so don't be late."

She nods her head and says, "Yes sir."

Good girl. I place my hand on the small of her back, shutting the door and leading her out of the front room and straight to the stairs. She's glancing around and taking it all in, but I have no intention of showing her anything other than the playroom today. Well, and the guest room later tonight since I know I'll be needing her in the morning.

I'm rushing her and I know that I am, but I need to get this first part out of the way and over with. We've wasted nearly an entire day, and I'm eager to start her training.

As I lead her up the stairs she walks with her head down, and her breathing comes in heavier.

"I want you to wait for me in this room," I say as I get to the second door on the left. She stands patiently as I open the door.

I wait for her to enter, letting her curiosity lead her in. Her steps are slow and hesitant, but she walks into the room and takes everything in. Her own desire leads her to the bed in the center of the room, her fingers running along the comforter.

I close the door as quietly as possible and watch as she walks over to the row of whips and punishment tools.

"Pick one." My command startles her as she gasps and turns around. Her slightly frightened look only makes me want her more.

"I want to know what you most enjoy, and what would be the best punishments as well." I walk over to her slowly as she nods her head and looks back at the wall of toys to choose from.

Her fingers gently brush the tails of a whip and I think she's going to choose it, but instead she moves to a simple paddle. I like both equally, and so I'm fine with that.

I take it from her trembling hands and set it on the bed. The cuffs are already attached to the frame, and the spreader is ready for her, too. I set up everything last night.

"I want to jump into our first session, Dahlia." Her stance is tense, and her breathing is coming in pants. When I finally get a chance to sink my fingers into her pussy I know she's going to be soaking wet for me. I can't fucking wait.

I start unbuckling my belt. And I give her a simple command. "Strip."

She starts to slowly and sensually remove her clothes, but I haven't the time for that. I want her too badly to enjoy a tease.

"Faster. I want you naked and ready for me when I come in here. You should be naked and kneeling next to the end of the bed. Go there now."

Her eyes widen, and she looks away as though she's embarrassed. As if she's done something wrong, and I don't like it. She didn't know my preferences, so she has no reason to feel self-conscious. Maybe it's the way I'm being short with her, I'm not certain, but if it is then she'll learn not to let it bother her. Or else she'll be miserable for the next few weeks.

She leaves her clothes in a pile on the floor, kicking out of her heels and walking quickly to the end of the bed to kneel.

Her chest rises and falls with each nervous breath. She sits on her heels, moving her knees slightly apart, her hands resting on her thighs. Her head is angled down. She has gorgeous posture for a Submissive. I step out of my clothes, keeping her waiting. The belt buckle falls noisily onto the floor and she jumps slightly, but doesn't look up. My eyes never leave her, waiting for her reaction.

"Have you used a safe word before?" I ask as I walk over in front of her, stroking my cock as I move. I'm already leaking precum with the need to be inside her hot mouth.

She gulps as she stares at my throbbing cock, forgetting to answer. I light up with the desire to correct her behavior, but she shakes her head and quickly adds, "No, sir." Although the fire to train her is dimmed by her obedience, I'm still on edge with need.

"Simply put, I'll test you. I'll push your boundaries and when I ask you where you are, you'll answer red for stop, yellow if you're getting close, or green if we're in safe territory."

She finally looks up at me with wide eyes and her lips parted with a question, but she quickly looks back down.

"Ask me," I tell her, stroking my dick again.

"What if-" she starts, but I interrupt her.

"Look at me when you speak," I snap out my words and it makes her jolt slightly as she looks up to meet my gaze. Her skin is bright red, and I love it. I love how on edge she is.

"What if you don't ask?"

I stare at her in wonder for a moment. "I should. But if I don't, you can speak up at any point." I crouch down in front of her, taking her chin in my hand and angling her lips closer to mine. "I'll be looking for your limits. I don't want to push you over the edge." Her eyes dart past me and shine with uncertainty, and I'm not quite sure why. I know she's never had a Dom, so that must be why. She just simply isn't prepared.

I stand up straight and tell her, "I'm going to show you what I mean." Her eyes glance at my cock as I stroke it again. Those beautiful hazel eyes are heated with lust. Her fingers dig into her thighs to keep from lifting her hands. She already knows a good bit of what's expected. I like that. I fucking love that she's trying to obey. But she's going to fail at some point, and I can't wait to discipline her.

"Open," I give her the simple command and she obeys, opening her mouth and breathing huskily as I put the head of my dick up to her mouth.

Fuck, she looks gorgeous. She bends her head forward, but I shake my head no and she quickly moves back to her previous position.

"Open wider," I tell her and she does her best, widening

her jaw for me as I ease my dick in past her lips. I spear my fingers through her hair and push myself in deeper. Her tongue massages the underside of my dick as I push in even farther. Her cheeks hollow as I fist her hair and move her up and down my length. She moans, and the vibrations makes my dick stir with need and my toes dig into the carpet.

I shove my dick into the back of her throat, feeling it close tightly around the head as she tries to swallow it. I don't pull back, instead I push in even deeper, watching as her eyes water and she struggles to take my short shallow pumps. She feels too good and the sight of her makes me want to cum this very second, but I'm not going to let that happen. Not yet.

Her fingers dig into her thighs and her throat tries to swallow me again, feeling like fucking heaven, but I know she's at her limit and I pull back. My hand is still fisted in her hair as she takes in a breath. As she inhales, I reach down and push my fingers between her thighs. She's fucking drenched.

"Go lie on the bed," I say and stroke my dick as she scrambles to do as she's told, still taking in deep breaths and wiping the spit away from her mouth.

She lies in the center of the bed with her hands at her sides. I crawl on top of her and straddle her waist, picking up one wrist and strapping her to one of the leather cuffs attached to the bed, and then securing the other wrist.

"Safe word," I say and watch her expression as I latch the buckle and test out the restriction on her wrists.

"Green," she answers quickly and confidently.

I crawl down her body and pull her down with me, sliding her along the sheets until her arms are stretched. She looks beautiful like this. Her pale rose nipples are pebbled and I lean down, sucking one into my mouth out of pure temptation. My fingers trail along the dip in her waist, testing her. Simply playing with her body for my enjoyment, and to test how reactive she is. She's quite responsive, which I enjoy, although I know many Doms don't. I'm grateful they haven't had a chance to taint her with their preferences.

I reach to the far end of the bed and attach the spreader to her right ankle. I look up her body and to her face to gauge her reaction as I attach her left ankle and snap the steel spreader open, widening her legs so she's completely exposed to me.

She sucks in a breath, and her glistening pussy clenches around nothing. She's completely helpless as I flip the spreader bar over, making her squeal as her arms cross and she lies on her belly. She breathes heavily into the pillow as I crawl up her body, leaving small open-mouth kisses up her sensitive skin and continuing playing with her. I finally reach her neck, and I graze my teeth along her skin and then nip her bottom lip.

She moans in the hot air between us.

"You're mine, treasure. To do whatever the fuck I want to do to you." I bite down on her earlobe and my dick presses into her side as she moans. "Is that what you want?" I ask her.

"Yes," she breathes the answer with lust and I bring my hand down hard on her ass. "Sir!" she's quick to yell out.

I chuckle as I sit up and flip her back over onto her ass with the flick of my wrist as I hold the spreader bar. I bring it closer to the headboard, folding her in on herself and attaching the locks to her ankles, so she's completely bared to me and unable to move.

Fuck, she looks so goddamn beautiful. Her breathing is the only thing I can hear as I shove two thick fingers into her tight cunt.

"Safe word," I ask her as I curl my fingers and roughly finger fuck her over and over.

"Green," she yells out desperately. She likes it rough; the harder and more forceful I am, the more her skin flushes and the sweeter the sounds are spilling from her lips.

I pull my fingers out and hold them up to my lips, taking a taste of her. I close my eyes and groan at the sweet flavor. I suck them clean as she watches me closely. I had intended to make her do it, but the heated look in her eyes as she watches my primal needs is addicting.

I grab her ass and move her slightly before lining my dick up with her pussy. I don't ask, and I don't give her any more warning than that before I slam my dick deep inside of her, the cuff buckles clanging against the frame of the bed and her scream of pleasure filling the room.

I don't give her time to adjust. Instead I fuck her savagely, taking everything I want from her. My blunt fingernails dig into the flesh of her ass as I groan out in an even voice I don't recognize, "Safe word."

"Green," she moans, arching her back. I move my hands to the small of her back and fuck her harder and deeper. She never shows any sign that it's too much as I hammer my hips against hers.

I lean forward and growl into the crook of her neck, "I wanna feel your tight pussy pop on my dick." I piston my hips over and over as she screams my name. She shouldn't be using my name in this room. But I don't have it in me to correct her. I'm too lost in pleasure and focused on finding her limits. "Now," I say and then bite down on her shoulder.

Fuck!

Her hot cunt spasms around my dick, practically choking it as I ride through her orgasm. I feel my balls draw up, and I have to pull out before I cum.

I gently rub her clit in circular motions, drawing out her release as I catch my breath.

Her chest and cheeks are a bright red, and her legs are shaking uncontrollably with pleasure. She fucking loves this.

I pull away and watch her calm, still bound to the bed. So far everything's going just as I wanted. She hasn't disappointed me in the least.

"When's the last time you've been fucked in your ass?" I ask her as I reach for the bottle of lube behind me. Her pussy is soaked, and there's a good bit of her arousal and cum on my dick that's leaked down to her ass, but I need to make sure I don't hurt her.

"A while," she whispers, her breath still coming in ragged pants. She gasps as I gently prod her ass, spreading the lube over her tight ring.

I gently push my middle finger in, and she pushes back. I fucking love that I won't have to work her ass up for me. I want her now. I want to cum in her ass right now.

Fuck, yes. My dick is aching with the need to be buried inside her again. I pump another finger into her ass and watch as she writhes on the bed.

That's all I need, I can't take any more.

"Yes," I hiss with pleasure as I sink deep into her ass and she claws at the cuffs around her wrists. I don't stop my slow thrust until I feel her ass completely surround my dick.

"Safe word?" I ask her from deep in my chest.

She's quiet with her head thrashing as she tries to stretch and get accustomed to my girth.

I pull out slowly, with a hint of a smile on my face, although I can't let her know. I'm hitting everything I wanted to with ease. And now I get to punish her.

She breathes heavily as I pull out of her and grab the spreader bar with my left hand, angling her so I have a better view of her ass cheek and pick up the paddle with my right.

Whack!

Her body bucks at the blow, but I have the spreader firm in my grasp and I'm not letting her move an inch.

"You need to answer me the second I ask you a question, Dahlia."

"Green," she says with nothing but lust in her voice, but it's too late. She needs to be punished.

I spank her ass with the paddle again, watching her jump slightly and pull against the binds, but it's useless. *Whack! Whack! Whack!* I smack the paddle against her reddened flesh over and over. "Safe word?" I ask her loudly so she can hear me over her gasps.

"Green!" she screams out, exposing her throat as she arches her neck. *Whack!* I smack the paddle flat across her ass harder than before, and she draws in a sharp breath. *Whack! Whack!* Her mouth opens in a silent "O" and I know the endorphins are finally running through her, making everything hotter and more pleasurable and intense.

"Safe word?" I ask her as I gently press my palm to her hot skin.

"Green," she moans softly with her brow scrunched. Good girl.

"You'll answer me the first time I ask you now, won't you?" I say as I debate on giving her another round to get more endorphins flowing.

"Yes, sir," she says breathlessly. Her nipples are pebbled and her words coated in lust.

I toss the paddle behind me, she doesn't need any more, and line my dick up. I'm not gentle as I slam into her tight asshole.

"Ah!" she screams out as I hammer into her. My hands grip her thighs as I pump my hips, watching her face for cues. She feels so fucking good. I knew it. I knew she'd feel like this.

I almost get lost in pleasure, but I can't just cum yet.

I fuck her ass harder and harder, the buckles of the cuffs clinking, the feet of the bed slamming on the ground and her strangled cries of pleasure fueling me to continue. It's a near violent and relentless pace, and I watch her face, waiting for the limit. I know she's going to need to say it. I need to hear her. I need to know I can trust her to tell me when it's too much.

I angle my hips and shove my thick cock all the way into her ass, my fingers digging into her ankles as I push into her to the hilt, filling her ass and making her scream. She pants out her breaths and tries to struggle against me, but it's useless. I hammer into her, pistoning my hips, pushing further on the side of pain.

I start to worry as she doesn't say it. She doesn't give me any indication that she's close to her limit. She wants this, she's enjoying the pleasure and pain blending into one, but I'm nearing my own limits. She isn't a red girl. There was no indication that she preferred pain in the meeting or the pamphlet.

My own breath comes in ragged as her face scrunches and I continue thrusting my hips into her tight hole.

"Yell-" she starts to say, craning her neck with her body

tensing. I still inside of her and bend down, moving under the spreader bar and kissing her lips sweetly.

"Good girl," I whisper against her lips as her face relaxes and I move easily in and out of her with slow deliberate thrusts only meant for pleasure. She opens her eyes slowly, and for a fraction of a second a spark ignites between us, something forceful I've never felt before. I'm quick to move away, regaining my position and roughly rubbing her throbbing clit with the rough pad of my thumb.

"Cum for me, treasure," I give her the command as my own orgasm slowly approaches, making my spine tingle and my toes curl. She closes her eyes and thrashes her head as I give her a quicker pace, fucking her ass and rubbing her clit to get her off.

But she's struggling to get there. My own is approaching, and I want her to cum again. I need that. I have to have her sated and finding her release with mine.

I pull my hand away from her pussy and her eyes pop open, looking back at me as I smack the back of my hand down hard across her clit. That does it. Her pussy spasms around nothing, and I thrust into her tight asshole over and over as the waves of my release finally crash through my body.

Yes!

My balls draw up, and I hold my breath as pleasure wracks through my body.

Fuck, she feels too fucking good.

I pump short, shallow thrusts into her ass as her body trembles beneath me and she screams out my name. Thick streams of hot cum leave me in waves as I bury myself as deep in her as I can and groan in utter pleasure.

I tighten my grip on her thigh as she trembles under me and I fill her with my cum.

When I finally pull away, breathless and sated, I do so gently, pulling out slowly and watching her body as she lies limp and still helplessly bound by the spreader and cuffs. Her head is laying to the side with her eyes closed, and goosebumps linger along her sensitized skin.

A part of me wants to take more from her, but she's exhausted and we need to cover more of my expectations. Soon I'll be able to torture the pleasure from her until it's nearly unbearable for her.

I climb off the bed and head to the en-suite for a warm cloth, leaving her just as she is while she calms her breathing.

When I get back with the warm, wet cloth, I'm gentle as I clean up every inch of her. Her body tenses and trembles. Her clit is still primed for more, and her ass is bright red from where the paddle hit her.

The bed groans under my weight as I unlock the spreader from the cuffs and ease her legs down onto the bed and unlock the shackles around her ankles. I massage a bit of life into her sore muscles before unlocking her wrists and doing the same with her arms.

Her breathing is steady as she curls slightly inward, still consumed in the intensity of her orgasm.

I pick her body up gently and place her on all fours at the end of the bed. Her bright red ass is high in the air.

Her eyes widen, and her breath hitches as she looks over her slender shoulder at me.

A rough chuckle vibrates up my chest as I walk over to get the cream mixed with a little aloe for her burning skin. I use a light touch as I apply it.

"You safe worded me," I say softly. "Good girl."

Her lips part and I know she has a question for me, but she's holding back.

"Speak. You need to be able to communicate with me, Dahlia."

"I'm happy you weren't angry with me." I pause in my motions and consider her.

"You think it would make me angry for you to tell me you were reaching your limits?" I shake my head with my lips turned down. "No, I'm happy I have a good understanding of your needs."

I put the cap back on the lotion, satisfied with her aftercare and add, "We suit each other well. I'm very pleased."

She hums softly at my praise. She's perfect and so obedient. I'm going to have to push her to disobey though since I know we both enjoyed the paddle.

"Just like this, treasure," I say, planting a kiss on the small of her back and running my hands down her thighs.

"Every day when I get home, you'll be waiting for me just like this."

"Not kneeling?" she asks weakly and then adds, "sir?"

I huff a small laugh and then stroke my dick, feeling it hardening for her again already.

I lower her hips and tease her cunt with the head of my dick. "No, I want you like this instead," I say and barely get the words out before I shove myself deep inside her again.

CHAPTER 12

DAHLIA

I wince as I take a seat on the back of the city bus on my way to my internship. My breath hisses between my teeth as the decadent pain heats my ass. I welcome it though. It's a reminder of last night. I stare out of the window, the images flashing before my eyes as the bus noisily roars to life and takes me away from campus. It's been a week of enduring Lucian as my Dom, and every day I love it more and more.

I'm running late because of finals, but I'm happy they're over with. One less thing to worry about.

My only problem now is that my ass is fucking sore as hell. Every time I do anything involving any kind of movement, I'm filled with slight discomfort. It's the good type of pain though - a reminder of how Lucian utterly and thoroughly dominated my body.

Call me a glutton for punishment, but I want more. Right fucking now.

I've spent all morning thinking about our filthy encounter, with aching desire. I'm already primed to go off and if my day was planned down to the minute, I'd probably need relief. I can't believe how many times Lucian got me off last night and how many times he came. I'm sure he was shooting blanks by the fourth time, but I was too wrapped up in ecstasy to notice.

Every time he took me harder, faster, taking from me with a ruthless need, I came violently. He was everything I wanted. It was perfect. But everything I've been running from smacked me hard in the face early this morning. I swallow thickly, the lust disappearing and the shame creeping in. He rolled over and pulled my back into his chest. He fucked me from behind, but he was tender. He was gentle. He kissed my neck, and I had to close my eyes and pretend. The pleasure stopped. No matter how much I wanted to, I couldn't get off. I feel shitty, having been so aroused moments before, and enjoyed being used for his pleasure. But then numb to him.

The truth is, I want more of his roughness. I've always needed that. My heart clenches and I pull away from the window, pulling my hobo bag into my lap and holding it against my chest. I feel hollow inside. How disturbed am I that he couldn't make me cum? I had to fake it when he told me to cum with him. For fuck's sake, I'm living a fantasy. But even this morning when he threw me on the bed and fucked me like I wanted, the only thing my body craved, I couldn't get the fact that I'm broken out of my head. Fuck, it hurts.

I feel sick about it. I just don't understand it. It makes me fear that I'll never be normal and that this experience will only serve to show how depraved and fucked up I am in the head. I bite the inside of my cheek and pull out my phone. I should call Dr. Andrews. I cringe at the thought. I know there's doctor-patient confidentiality, but what's she going to think about this *arrangement*? Whore. I lean my head back against the seat as the bus goes over a bump and jostles me slightly. She's going to think I'm whoring myself out. I run my hand down my face and try to ignore those thoughts that keep me weighed down with guilt and shame. All I need to do is concentrate on the way I felt alive under him.

I'm pulled out of my musing as the bus comes to a stop in front of the Explicit Designs building. Wincing, I get up from my seat and head inside, swallowing the lump that's growing in my throat. In the lobby, I try to pick up speed, but I'm forced to take it slow. I don't want to draw attention to my awkward gait.

Damn you, Lucian.

A small smile accompanies me as I walk slowly, reveling in the slight sting that's directly connected to my throbbing clit. It takes me a while, but I make it up to my office without incident. Once inside the not-nearly-as-private-as-I-need-it-to-be office, I take off my coat, and set it down on my glass-top desk, letting out a shiver. It's brutal outside.

Which reminds me; it's winter break, and my tuition is due. At first the reminder sends a jolt of worry through me, but then I remember the money. I have enough coming to me at the end of the month to eliminate my debt and pay off my final semester's tuition. The thought should fill me with shame and trigger the whore comments I've been hearing in my head, but it doesn't. I know what I'm doing some people might consider degrading, but I don't really care. I would want this regardless of the money. That has to count for something.

I set my purse down on the desk and bring my cup of coffee to my lips. I blow on it out of habit, but it's cold by now. I don't mind though; I just need the caffeine to get me through the day. I check my email and then get started working on Debra's scheduling for her upcoming fashion show. I spend most of the day doing clerical work, getting up several times to go to the bathroom to apply aloe vera to my sore ass cheeks. Lucian told me to, and each time there's less and less of a sting that accompanies it.

Around closing time, I get a surprise when Carla, who I haven't seen all day, pops her head in the doorway, causing me to jump in my seat. I put my hand to my chest and breathe out a slight sigh of relief.

"Hey chica, how's your day going?" She's gorgeous today in tight red jeans that hug her curves and a white button-up shirt, complete with glossy red heels. I absolutely love the outfit. It makes her look like she's ready for a red-hot, sexy Christmas. All she's missing is a red Santa cap.

Carla grins at the slight pain on my face from moving in my seat. She knows exactly where it's coming from, too. The bitch. "Just fabulous," I reply, with a blush heating my cheeks. I want to tell her everything, but I'm nervous about the NDA. I should ask Lucian. Or maybe I shouldn't. ...shit. I don't know what to do.

"If not for the sore ass?" Carla jokes. It's honestly not that bad. It's certainly acted as a reminder of who I belong to though.

I scowl at her, but I can only hold it for a second before I laugh. "Shut up! Please." I have to resist rolling my eyes. "You wouldn't be talking if you were in my shoes."

Carla chuckles, shaking her head and then walks in, her heels clicking with each step, and sits down across from me. "Bet you I would. You forget honey, I'm a pro at being a Sub and have had many rough sessions." She smirks deviously. "Let's just say my ass can take a heavy pounding."

I huff out a short chuckle. It's weird hearing Carla talk like this, even after all this time. I would've never guessed she was such a sexual fiend before she revealed her secret to me. I suspect it's going to take some time before I ever get used to it. *If* I ever get used to it.

She's so different here at work in front of others. It's like two split personalities. But then again, people would probably say the same about me if they knew I was a member of Club X.

"Well?" Carla asks, pulling me out of my thoughts.

I frown with confusion. "Well what?"

She smacks her hand on the desk. "Details! You said you'd give me details." She leans forward and places her chin in her palm, greedy for the juicy gossip.

I hesitate. I'm not sure I want to tell her everything, especially the part about me not being able to get off. Part of me is screaming to confide in her. She's obviously a woman who would understand, right? But no one has ever understood. No one. Not my ex, not my mother. They knew, but they didn't understand. It's a problem. It's the only thing on the tip of my tongue. I want advice. I want help. I take in a short breath, but I can't say the words.

I try to school my expression and not show the pain that's squeezing my chest. Everything was perfect yesterday. I should be happy. I should be thrilled to tell her about Lucian. Instead all I can think about is the one moment this morning that was anything but alright.

"Dah?" Carla sounds concerned and my eyes snap to her, shutting down the negative thoughts. "Did he hurt you?" she barely breathes the words, fear evident in her eyes.

"No!" I'm quick to get that thought out of her head. I shake my head as I say, "No, no, it was... unbelievable." She looks at me for a moment, taking in my expression and posture.

Taking a deep breath, I tell her everything about this past week, except that one moment early this morning.

Carla grins, her chest heaving, her breathing ragged. She doesn't appear to notice my anxiety and seems to have gotten worked up over my tale. "I'm so glad you liked it. Sounds like Lucian really knows his stuff." She shakes her head with wonder. "And you safe worded him and everything."

"Is that bad?" I ask her in a hushed voice. I didn't want to. I wanted to be perfect for him, but it was just too much. He said it was good though. I really believed him when he told me he wanted me to tell him if I was at my limit.

Carla shakes her head, her eyes shining with a hint of awe and says, "No, it's good to know each other's boundaries."

Her words summon the image of Lucian spanking me, leaving red marks on my ass and my breathing quickens. *That.* That power. That control. It's that which I crave above all else.

"My only problem is..." I snap my mouth shut, shocked at how close I came to thinking out loud. Holy fuck. How did I almost tell her? Is that even a boundary? I pick at my nails and look past her and out the window of my little office.

Carla eyes me curiously. "Your only problem is what?"

Her eyes on me force me to look back at her, my mind racing with excuses, unsure what to say. I shouldn't tell her. But it's right on the tip of my tongue. Maybe I should give her a chance and just tell her. She might understand.

But if she doesn't? What then?

That thought alone scares me above all else, and it hardens my position. I'm not telling Carla shit.

"Nothing," I say, shaking my head and flashing her a nervous smile. "It's nothing really."

Carla isn't buying it. "C'mon," she gestures with a manicured finger at me. "You can't just leave me hanging like that. You have to tell me."

"No," I say firmly. "Really, it's nothing." Her ensuing scowl causes me to sigh and I say, "Fine. I was just going to say I wish it didn't have to end in a month." I'm surprised by how easily that lie came out.

Carla chuckles, and I'm filled with relief. She bought my lie. "Girl, with a man as good looking as Lucian, I don't blame you." She snaps her fingers. "Oh, which reminds me!" She watches her finger as she taps on the glass desktop. "Do you think Lucian will be bringing you to the club?" I don't know how to respond. "I just think it would be good for you if you had time in the club, with other Subs and such."

I freeze, caught off guard.

"Bruce did it for me," she adds. She seems really nervous and I honestly feel the same way. He *owns* me. I don't know what the rules are outside of the playroom.

"I don't know," I say slowly.

"Just ask him," she says finally. "It's just that, sometimes it's easy to get sucked into a fantasy," she says as her eyes flash with a sadness I've never seen. "And I don't want you getting hurt."

I stare back at her with a knot growing in the pit of my stomach and reply, "Trust me, I don't want to get hurt either.

CHAPTER 13

LUCIAN

I need to rein in my anger before I get home, but all I'm thinking about is taking this tension out on my sweet Dahlia. I know she must be sore from the past two weeks, but I'm not going to be able to hold back.

I *need* her.

Just the thought of sinking deep inside her makes me relax.

I've been dealing with one problem after another all day. I clench my teeth as I relive every tiresome phone call from public relations and my lawyer. My ex-wife. She had the nerve to laugh at me during our call. I know she just wanted to get under my skin. I tried to hide my irritation, but she knows she got to me. I let her in, and all she did was find my weaknesses. She wants to exploit them now. I imagine she's run out of the small fortune she was awarded right around this time last year. It took over two years for our divorce to be finalized. She wouldn't settle on a perfectly reasonable sum; she wouldn't settle for anything other than everything.

And I bent over backward and gave it to her.

That was my mistake. Not the first, though. Marrying her was my first mistake. But giving her what she wanted only proved to her that she could get more.

But I won't allow it.

The phone rings in my pocket, and I grit my teeth at the sound. My temples pound with each of the incessant rings.

I don't want to answer it; I want to get home. To my treasure.

I breathe out deep and think, *soon*. Soon I'll be lost inside of her. Where I belong.

I hit the small center button on my dashboard and lean back in my leather seat, twisting my hands around the steering wheel.

"Stone," I answer smoothly. Never show emotion. I've learned better than to let them see they can affect me. Tricia is the perfect example of why I can never let them know how I feel. They call me ruthless, heartless. Well, they made me that way.

"Mr. Stone, it's Jackson." Jackson Harris, my lawyer. "We have a situation." I cringe at the ease in his voice. He doesn't have a situation. He gets paid regardless. If my ex could afford him, he'd be on her team right now. He's not loyal to me. Neither is my PR team, but I'll pay them whatever they need to get this shit dealt with.

"And that is?" I ask as though I don't already know. Tricia's been harassing the office, calling me nonstop. I've gotten her message, but apparently she hasn't received mine.

"Tricia's refuting the legitimacy of the NDA."

I let his words sink in. During our divorce, she agreed to sign the NDA and legally cannot discuss any matters pertaining to our relationship during any period of time, married or otherwise. "I fail to see how that's an issue. She's contractually-"

He cuts me off, "She can refute it, although she has no footing."

"Then how is this a problem?"

"I've received several calls from Andrea, and it is apparent that Tricia has reached out to several editorials and is taking bids for her story." My blood runs cold as I drive down the highway. My heart pumps harder in my chest and I try to focus and not be consumed with the anger that's barely contained.

Her story. As though she's anything other than a gold digger. I gave her everything, and the moment she found someone else, she left me. She thought she had it made with me. But I worked too much. Always bitching that I needed to make more, but be home more. She was impossible to please.

I tried. I fucking tried. I slam my fist down on the wheel. At least karma bit her in the ass and the asshole she cheated on me with left her. It would've been better if I could have proved that she was cheating. Then she would have walked away with far less.

I take in a deep breath, pulling off of the interstate and getting closer to my penthouse.

"She has nothing to lose, Lucian. We can sue her afterward, but the damage will be done." I swallow thickly, hating that one mistake so many years ago can continue to cause me damage.

"And what do you suggest?" I ask him.

"We can pay her, or the magazines, but I imagine she'd be cheaper." I scoff and look out of the window as I drive into the private garage and key in my personal PIN. I check the time, it's six forty. My little treasure should be waiting for me.

"She's not getting anything. I refuse to pay her one cent."

Just as I say the words, the sound of an incoming call comes through the background.

"It will be expensive not to pay her, Mr. Stone. We can always pay now and sue later." His tone holds a hint of a warning, letting me know he doesn't approve, but I don't give a fuck. He works for me, and I don't care how much money I have to spend to make sure she doesn't profit off a damn thing from me anymore.

"No. She gets nothing." I end the call and answer the next, pulling my black R8 in next to the Aston Martin. I'm on the fourth floor of the garage. It's private and all mine. I glance around the space as I answer, "Stone."

"Mr. Stone, this is Andrea from the agency, do you have a moment to speak with me?"

I pinch the bridge of my nose and wish I could ignore these problems. Public relations is a pain in my ass.

A long inhale calms me slightly as I say, "I'm listening."

"Given the current climate, I've been working with Alena and we feel it may be best if we were to combat the possibility of your ex's story being released with a different form of press."

I open my mouth to remind her that in my opinion, no press is good press. I don't want to be seen anywhere. I can't even stand the business articles from Forbes and Business Insider. I'm not interested.

"I understand that you prefer to stay out of the limelight, so to speak, but in my professional opinion…" she pauses on the phone and I find myself watching the digital dash, waiting for her to continue. "May I be frank with you, Mr. Stone?"

"Yes." I prefer if everyone were frank so I didn't have to deal with fake bullshit.

"Your wife has held this over your head for years, and her story is going to come out whether she profits from it or not, doesn't matter. She's going to go through with this. I think it's best that we create an appearance now that will refute the picture she intends to paint."

I swallow thickly, staring straight ahead through the windshield at the grey cylinder blocks of the garage. I'm numb to this. There's nothing that she can really do to hurt me. I glance at the elevator. I just want to get upstairs to my penthouse and go straight to the playroom.

A small smile kicks my lips up. She'll be waiting for me like a good girl. Just like yesterday and every day these past two weeks. It's time to give her some real training. My fingers itch to touch the thick coarse fibers of the rope that's already laying on the bed. She's going to get a lesson in saying please and thank you today, and I can hardly wait.

"I think it would be best to create the impression that you're in a committed and loving relationship. We all love couples. So much more so than a nasty divorce. Weddings are the best sellers."

My eyebrows raise at her comment. She's delusional if she thinks that shit's going to happen. "I'm not interested in a PR stunt, Andrea."

"I'm only saying, what if you were to be seen in a romantic setting and paparazzi happened to take your picture? And let's say that the picture happened to be leaked, along with a story that you confirmed to be true. Well if that situation were to occur, it would go a long way in making your ex look like a villain and you as a prince charming that the public is rooting for."

It's quiet for a moment as I consider her request.

"It will make you look relatable. In fact, it may be better than the story she's selling," she adds with a bright and cheery tone. "Just a thought."

"Fine," I finally say with my fingers on the key in the ignition.

"Wonderful," Andrea's tone remains upbeat. I have a feeling she must have real assholes for clients since she's never bothered by my tone. "Shall we send someone out for you?"

"No," I'm quick to cut her off. I have my treasure, and I think she'd enjoy it. I pause as I realize I hadn't thought twice about whether or not it should be Dahlia. I can imagine how I'd tease her under the table. Yes. I have to remember cameras will be watching, but I'm going to enjoy myself.

"Thank you, Andrea. I'll have my reservations for this evening sent to you."

"No need, Mr. Stone. You're all set at the Ritz; a table's been reserved for you at any time you choose."

I huff a humorless laugh. "You pay us well, Mr. Stone," Andrea says. "I have faith in this plan."

I don't, but at least I have my treasure waiting for me.

CHAPTER 14

DAHLIA

A shiver snakes down my limbs as my thighs tremble from exertion, my ass stuck high into the air. I've been waiting in this position for what feels like forever. It's a bit uncomfortable, but it's how he wants me. *My sir.* He's coming for me. And he expects me to be ready to take him. *All of him.*

My breathing becomes heavy, labored, as I keep my hands firmly planted against the lush mattress. I want to be perfect for him. I need to please him and make sure I obey. The only thing he's asked of me is to wait for him just like this. And I can do that. I did it yesterday.

My body trembles again, my ass trembling with a chill, my pussy clenching with insatiable need. *Fuck.* I can hardly wait.

Keeping myself balanced, I glance around the room. My

clothes are in a neat pile on a chair in the corner, but Lucian isn't here yet. *Where is he?* I want him here now. Ravaging me. Dominating me for everything I'm worth.

I turn my head back toward the wall, concentrating on keeping my ass suspended in the air. I'll wait however long it takes for him to get here. I need him to see me like this the moment he walks in. My nipples pebble as I imagine him walking down the hall toward this master suite, dressed in one of his expensive business suits, his shirt unbuttoned, his tie loosened, looking sexy as fuck. *Ready* to fuck.

I let out a groan, my pussy clenching repeatedly on thin air, wishing his cock was there. Another groan escapes my lips as I imagine him behind me, fucking me mercilessly, his blunt nails digging into my hips as he thrusts harder and deeper.

I'm so horny, I have the overpowering urge to reach down and rub my pussy. But I know I'm not supposed to. I scissor my thighs, craving some friction. Just the tiniest bit. It's a battle, and I'm almost about to give in to the desire to touch myself, when I hear the sound of the door creaking open.

Relief flows through my abdomen as excitement causes my limbs to shudder. *Yes.*

I go perfectly still at the sound of Lucian's voice, keeping my ass right where he told me to.

"Treasure," I hear him growl behind me, his deep baritone filling the room and making my clit throb even more.

I tremble slightly, feeling my breath quickening. "Yes sir?"

I ask breathlessly. Just being in his presence is such a huge turn-on, knowing what's to come. What he's going to do to me. My whole body has come alive with desire.

I hear the sound of his muted footsteps against the plush carpeting and I fight the urge to turn around to catch a glimpse of him. He hasn't given me permission.

The bed creaks as he gets on it and goosebumps rise along my skin, traveling from the base of my spine toward my shoulders and down my front. A second later I feel his hot breath on my ass cheeks and I know he's level with my ass, eyeing my glistening pussy. My heart begins to pound like a war drum, beating so hard that Lucian probably hears it.

I close my eyes in anticipation, my breathing ragged and shallow as I wait for him to bury his face in my pussy and then make me beg for more.

"I asked you to wait for me here and to be still, treasure," Lucian growls from behind me, his hot breath grazing my pussy and causing it to clench even harder. He puts a hand on either side of my ass and spreads me farther apart. My eyes widen, and my fingers dig into the mattress.

I buck forward slightly, the feel of his breath on me making me shiver uncontrollably. Oh my God. He's driving me crazy, and he knows it. Why won't he just put that mouth on my pussy and take me by force?

"I did, sir," I weakly protest. I'm practically trembling with exhaustion from holding this position for so long. For him.

"No, treasure," I hear him say as I feel his fingers lightly touch my mound, gliding along the slick, swollen flesh. I groan softly as I let his fingers dip inside and explore my sore walls. I feel a little discomfort that makes me wince, but it mixes in with the pleasure and I want more. Much more. My neck arches, and I bite down on my lip to keep from moaning. "You didn't."

He doesn't give me more, though. I gasp as he pulls his fingers away and I instantly miss his touch.

The bed creaks as Lucian crawls off of it and walks over to the nightstand. I sneak a peek to the side. I can see him now, and he looks just like I imagined him; his shirt unbuttoned at the chest, his tie loosened. And he has a huge fucking bulge pressing against his expensive slacks, dying to be let out. My mouth waters at the sight.

I watch as Lucian walks over to the side of the room, messing with something in a drawer before standing in front of the whips and canes. *Uh-oh.* My heart begins pounding like a sledgehammer as I read Lucian's body language. He means business.

"You were supposed to be still, treasure," he growls ominously, "and for the last five minutes you have been anything but still." Moving slowly, deliberately, he picks up a riding crop. He walks back over to the bed, dragging out each step, his face an impenetrable mask. My heart flutters, knowing what's coming next as he moves out of view behind me.

The bed creaks again and then everything goes still. *Silence.* I strain my ears, listening for Lucian's breathing, but all I can make out is my heart pounding between my ears.

Smack!

I buck forward as pain stings my right ass cheek and a soft cry escapes my lips. Immediately, I feel Lucian probing my pussy, his finger lathered with a cooling gel. My eyes close from the soothing relief. But it's temporary.

Smack! Smack! Smack!

I buck forward again, my head almost slamming into the headboard, crying out with pain and pleasure. Lucian continues to probe my pussy, my ass on fire from his brutal slaps. It hurts, but it feels *so good* at the same time. My body's alive with pleasure, wanting more but also wanting to get away. It takes everything in me to be good for him and obey. I have to stay still, but it's so fucking hard when my instincts are screaming at me to move.

"Are you going to listen, my treasure?"

"Yes," I say weakly, my limbs trembling with need, resisting the urge to angle my pussy as his fingers barely touch my throbbing clit. I'm so close.

Lucian strokes several fingers against my G-spot, nearly fisting me and causing me to gasp and white lights to dance in my vision. "Yes what?"

"Yes, sir!" I yell as my body threatens to fall over the high cliff of pleasure.

Smack! Smack!! The relentless smacks continue, and the pain turns to something else. Instead of moving away, I find my body eager for the next. *Smack! Smack!*

He slaps the riding crop against my ass again and I cry out once more. I feel pressure building inside of my core. I'm going to cum all over his fucking fingers if he keeps this up. My cheeks burn with embarrassment at how much I want his punishment. How much I crave and need it.

Suddenly, Lucian's hands are gone from my pussy and disappointment flows through my body. I was so close. I'm breathless, and my body weak with need and exhaustion.

"Your punishment is over," Lucian declares, making me even more upset. My heart tightens, and I find myself feeling unstable and weak. My ass hurts as he shifts his position.

I have the urge to protest, my lips parting, but nothing coming out. This was my punishment. I knew I should have been still. I should have controlled it. I close my eyes and try to ignore how upset I am.

"Thank you," I say, trying to keep my voice neutral and hide my disappointment.

"Thank you what?" he asks menacingly.

"Sir!" I say quickly. "Thank you, sir."

He's suddenly pressed against me, his breath hot on my neck. Behind me, I can feel his hard cock pressing up against my sore ass through his silk slacks. My pussy pulses in tandem with the blood that's pumping through his huge dick.

"Good girl," he whispers in my ear, his hand snaking around my waist and up my chest to clamp down on a hard nipple. "Now when I tell you to be still, will you be still?"

I hold in a moan as he gently pinches my nipple to the point that a gasp is forced from me. The sensation is directly linked to my throbbing clit. And again I feel on edge. "Yes, sir," I whisper, immediately turned on again, and nodding my head.

He gently kisses my shoulder and strokes my back. "You will, treasure." He releases me and gets up off the bed and frustration laces through me. I feel cheated somewhat. I want him back.

Keeping my expression neutral, I watch as he walks over to the corner and grabs my clothes out of the chair.

"Is this all you have?" he asks, looking down at the black skirt and cream blouse I'd worn on the way over and examining it.

Anxiety courses through me. I know they're not the most expensive clothes, but it's the best outfit I have.

Not knowing what to say, I give him a slight nod.

"When I ask a question," he growls, narrowing his eyes slightly at me, "I expect a verbal response."

I force it from my lips. "Yes, sir."

He looks down at the pile again and I can tell he's not pleased. A feeling of worthlessness touches my chest. I don't know why, but his disdain for my clothes makes me feel like shit. Like I'm not good enough. I hate it.

"It will have to do," Lucian says. "For tonight only. But after today, I'll need the sizes you wear so you'll be prepared for next time."

My face crinkles in confusion. He told me to be naked.

"We're going out, treasure," Lucian announces, tossing my outfit down the chair and moving his hands to the belt wrapped around his waist. He begins walking over to the bed while undoing his belt, his eyes on me, burning with an intensity that causes my skin to prickle. He gets his belt off and tosses it to the side, and then he pulls his slacks down around his ass, gripping his massive, swollen, throbbing cock in his hand and stroking it as he moves forward.

"But first things first," he growls, as he climbs onto the bed behind me, lines his huge dick up with my pussy... And plunges it deep inside with enough force to make me cry out.

Chapter 15

Lucian

Dahlia's blouse is loose on her and the wind blows it easily, pressing the thin fabric against her skin. The night is bitter cold, but all she has is a thin cardigan and a cream chiffon blouse. Her skirt covers her legs to her knees, but I imagine she's going to be cold.

I don't have a single item for a woman in this house. I should've been more prepared, but I had no intention of taking her out. Next time I'll be ready. I've already sent a text to Linda with Dahlia's sizes and everything I want for her. The thought takes me off guard that there will even be a next time. But I can't deny that I'm already thinking about taking her out again. Just the mention of dinner made her obviously happy.

I love the look on her face, and I want to keep her satisfied.

I know Madam Lynn has extended contracts in the past, so perhaps my Dahlia will be happy enough with the same arrangements.

I slip my jacket off my shoulders and place it around hers even though we aren't outside yet. She turns in the foyer, her heels clicking on the marble floors to look at me.

"I'll be alright," she says sweetly.

"That's not the correct response, my treasure," I leave a small note of admonishment to linger and she recognizes it although it's mostly meant to be playful.

"Thank you, sir." The soft blush to her cheeks makes her look innocent.

My fingers itch to reach out to her, but I resist. I know it's harder on Submissives to see the lines between a traditional relationship and what we have.

Dahlia's doing so well though. Especially for someone who's never participated in this lifestyle. "How are you enjoying this so far?" I ask as I slip my wallet into my back pocket and grab the keys off of the table.

"This?" she asks me, gesturing between the two of us.

A smile is forced onto my lips at her confusion. "Yes, Dahlia," I open the door and splay my hand on her lower back to lead her out, "how are you enjoying our arrangement?" I lock the door behind us and pull out my phone to send a text to Andrea letting her know we're leaving.

"I'm liking it so far," she says softly, the color intensifying in her cheeks. The sight of her shy beauty captivates me. I've loved every minute of pushing her boundaries and exploring the curves of her body.

"Good." I smile down at her and she rewards me with a sweet soft hum as she rocks back and forth on her heels, waiting for me to lead her away.

"You're excited for dinner?"

"I am," she replies and her smile widens. My chest swells with pride that I can put that beautiful look on her face.

My hand rests gently on her lower back and I lead her along.

She's quiet as we walk down the hallway and get into the elevator. The lighthearted feelings wane as I think about where we're going. It's late, but the paparazzi will be there, Andrea assures me in her text back. We won't even know they're there. A late-night candlelit dinner for two in a private room. It should be enough to satisfy the PR firm.

I clear my throat and consider what Dahlia will think of this. She needs to know this is a stunt and nothing more, but the thought of telling her the truth sends a prickle of unease down my skin. I don't want her to know any more than she has to. I also don't want her to be disappointed. She's genuinely happy, and I don't want to take that away.

"We'll be dining alone tonight." I have to set the ground rules for her. This isn't a date. I'm not an eligible bachelor. This is simply a dinner that she's attending with me as a Submissive, although, things will obviously be different.

"The rules are different outside the playroom, Dahlia," I tell her as I key in the code in the elevator chambers to take us to my floor of the garage.

She huffs a small laugh and her eyes slowly rise to meet mine. "I'm not even sure I know the rules in the playroom," she says softly.

Something about the look in her eyes makes me weak for her.

"Of course you do. You're perfect in the playroom, treasure," I say and cup her chin in my hand and run my thumb along her lower lip. They beg me to kiss her, but there are lines I'm not yet ready to cross. I don't want to lead her on, and this is already pushing it.

"You submit, and do your best to obey. You accept your punishment and best of all, you enjoy it." I release her as the elevator stops and lead the way out.

"That's all I ask of you, but when we're outside of the playroom, it's going to be far more difficult." She walks quickly to stay beside me as I stride toward the grey metal key box on the wall. The key to the penthouse opens it, and I pick out the Porsche 911. It's sleek and I want something different for tonight. Something hotter.

I eye my treasure. She looks beautiful, but she's dressed as if she could be my secretary or my assistant. I don't want anyone mistaking her for anything other than what she is. She's mine.

Tomorrow I'll have the clothes sent to her place. Enough

for a few dates at least. The idea of changing the rules and bringing our play out into the public is thrilling. It's new and different, and a challenge.

"Do you think you can play by a new set of rules, Dahlia?" I ask her.

She meets my gaze and nods, "Yes, sir."

"That's the first change." She pulls the jacket a little tighter around her shoulders. The wind is harsh as it blows into the cement garage.

She stares at me with those gorgeous hazel eyes flashing with a hint of uncertainty. "You'll call me Lucian when we're in public. And you're to act as though we're a couple."

"I can do that," she says thoughtfully.

My skin chills as I lead her to the red sports car and open the door. She walks quietly by my side, absorbing my words. I'm not interested in blurring these lines, and it may be difficult for her to remember what this is between us.

"Thank you," she says as she slips into the passenger seat. I wait until she's fully inside to gently shut the door.

My gut twists in my stomach knowing I'm leading myself to paparazzi. They're leeches and I hate the thought that I'm relying on them for this PR stunt, but if it works in my favor, I'll suffer through it.

I close my door and press the start button, the car purring to life. I glance at Dahlia and her legs have goosebumps, she's nearly shivering, huddled inside of my jacket. I click on the heated seats, but the heat itself will have to wait until the car heats.

"The rules are simple, Dahlia." I glance at her and then back onto the road. "You act as though we're a couple, just be mindful that people will be watching, even when you think no one is." I readjust in my seat and consider my next words, "Be respectful to me as your Dom. I know this is new to you, but you understand what that means, don't you?" I watch her from the corner of my eye.

"I think so," she answers hesitantly.

"Go on then."

"A Submissive is supposed to treat her Dominant with respect."

"As should a Dominant to his Submissive," I respond easily. I'm surprised by the flash of shock on her face and how her sweet lips part. "You don't agree?"

"I-" she starts to answer, but she doesn't finish her statement.

"Tell me about why you enjoy this, Dahlia." I keep my eyes on the road, but I'm fully focused on my treasure. It's important to me that we're on the same page here. I keep forgetting she's never done this before. That everything is new and different.

"I enjoy..." her voice trails off and she looks out of the window, tucking her hair back as she clears her throat. "I enjoy it when you're rough with me." She whispers her words, and the soft sounds makes my dick harden in my pants.

"I enjoy that, too," I tease her. "But this is more than just rough sex," I add.

"Yes," she answers diligently, nodding her head. "It's about me submitting all things and giving you control of the situation."

I wait for her to say more, but she doesn't. "And for you to trust that I know what you need, and that I'll provide it for you." I hold her gaze as we stop at a red light. Waiting for her to acknowledge that.

"Right," she says softly although there's no conviction in her voice.

"You've never had a relationship like ours before? But you've had boyfriends I assume?" It sounds odd to say the term boyfriend. I never much liked the word.

"I have."

"And would you call them dominant?" I ask her.

Her forehead pinches and she shakes her head slightly. "No. I wouldn't." She puts a finger to her lip and seems to truly consider what I'm asking.

"Tell me what you're thinking."

"My last... my ex." I drive easily, listening to her tell me about her experience. "He didn't really know how to help me in ways that I needed him to." It's a rather cryptic response, but I respect her privacy if she's not willing to divulge any more information.

"And you communicated your needs, but they weren't fulfilled. You couldn't trust him to take care of you in that way?"

"Right," she nods her head, "so yeah, I wouldn't say he was my Dominant. He didn't know how to be," her voice is soft and coated with the sound of realization. "He couldn't be my Dom."

"Is that why it didn't last?" I ask her. I'm curious. The conversation itself has made me want to know more.

"He just didn't understand." She answers with a sadness I wasn't expecting.

"What's that?"

"Hmm?" she hums.

"What didn't he understand?"

"I'd rather not talk about it, if that's alright?" The shyness and sadness mix in her eyes. Also apprehension.

"That's fine, treasure. You can keep a few secrets."

"My point was I respect your needs and your submission, and you do the same for me and my dominance. It's about trust, respect and communication."

I pull through the valet at the Ritz-Carlton and put the car in park so I can look at her. "Do you think I don't respect you, Dahlia?"

I ask her in all seriousness. I respect her and her submission. I know her needs, and what she enjoys. We share the same desires, so it's been extremely easy for me to fall into the dominant role in our relationship and fulfill her needs, but maybe I've missed something.

I lean forward and take her chin in my hand, tilting her lips to mine and planting a small chaste kiss against them.

"Don't forget for even one second, that every time I smack my hand across your ass, it's because I know you need it." I nip her bottom lip and then whisper, "Every time I fuck you until you can't breathe, it's because I know you want it." Her eyes close, and her lips part with lust. I reach my hand down and let my fingers play along the thin fabric of her underwear. "I give you want you want, I respect your needs, I cherish them."

"And you'll do the same for me, won't you, treasure?"

"Yes, sir," she whispers with lust.

"Ah, ah," I say as I pull away, turning the car off and pulling the key out. "Right now, it's 'yes, Lucian.'"

CHAPTER 16

DAHLIA

Every time I fuck you until you can't breathe, it's because I know you need it.

Lucian's words repeat in my mind as I climb out of his sports car, my breath catching in my throat as I take in the gorgeous view. Holding the door for me, Lucian gives me a boyish grin as a young valet dressed in a black suit and gold vest jogs up to us and hastily greets Lucian with a slight nod, asking him for the keys to the car.

"This is beautiful," I breathe, turning to Lucian and shaking my head. The valet grabs the keys from Lucian, grinning at the sports car like a kid at Christmas, before running around to the driver's side and jumping in. "I've never been taken to a place like this. Ever." I turn back and take in the restaurant with awe, admiring the scenic view. The building, which is cut of exquisite grey stone and has gleaming tall glass windows adorning the front, sits back on a terrace overlooking a beautiful lake. Floodlighting brightens the entire area, showcasing every inch of the grandmaster masonry. Intricately designed stamped concrete steps lead up to the entrance, a sparkling water fountain with ambient lighting rests at the center of the plaza, and a fancy balustrade runs up along each side. The full moon looms in the starry night sky, milky white light reflected against the water, making the scene even more romantic.

I watch in wonder as men in expensive suits and ties walk up the steps with women dressed in absolute finery on their arms. The gowns these ladies are wearing look like they cost a fortune, dazzling jewels and all, and it makes me feel more than a little self-conscious.

No wonder Lucian wasn't pleased by my outfit, I think to myself, glancing down at my outfit that seems drab compared to the others. *He's accustomed to seeing women wearing all this.*

Lucian is enjoying my shock, watching me with obvious amusement. "I thought you might like it," he says, splaying a hand across the small of my back. "But come, I think you'll enjoy the inside even more."

Breathless, I allow him to lead me up the steps to the restaurant, and I try to appear confident like all the other women around me. Like I belong on Lucian's arm. But it's hard. I can't stop worrying about people looking at me and thinking that I look out of place. Glancing around, no one seems to be paying us any mind, and the pleasant sounds of the waterfall take the edge off my anxiety.

Unconsciously I reach for Lucian's hand, wanting to feel security and comfort, and then snatch it back, fearful that I might be crossing the line. *Shit.* I didn't mean to do that. But isn't that what Lucian wants me to do? Pretend I'm his girlfriend? It's confusing, and my emotions and anxiety are getting the best of me.

I bite my lower lip nervously, glancing over at Lucian. He doesn't seem to have noticed my misstep and even places his hand on my right hip, guiding me up the last of the steps leading to the terrace.

Inside I'm completely blown away by the ritzy, upscale setting. The high-ceilinged room is a splash of gold and white, filled with luxury seating and high-class booths. There are several crowded bars on either side of the room, manned by attractive bartenders in deluxe suits. Delicate music seems to float to my ears from nowhere and a delightful scented fragrance tickles my nose. The walls are adorned with gold lights made up of gorgeous patterns that blend in with everything else, and on the back wall, the floor-to-ceiling windows provide a breathtaking view of the moonlit lake. The room is filled with the ultra-wealthy, the din of their chatter almost making me dizzy. I take it all in with a sharp breath. The seating, the lighting, the ambience--all of it is done to perfection.

"This is incredible," I say just above a murmur, unable to find a better word, my nervousness returning. I've never been somewhere like this in my entire life, and I feel totally out of my element. I step closer to Lucian and cling to his arm, wishing I could shrink and hide behind him as we move through a crowd of finely dressed couples toward the waiting area.

"I'm happy you like it." Lucian seems unconcerned with my anxiety and even wraps his arm around my waist as a waiter immediately approaches us. My cheeks redden at how Lucian is acting like I'm his property, and I have to take a moment to remember that he's doing this for show. I can't enjoy this too much. I can't get used to this either.

The waiter nods his head at Lucian, his eyes taking me in for a moment and then going back to Lucian. "Right this way, Mr. Stone. Your reservation is ready."

The waiter leads us over to a luxurious booth in a secluded corner and I try to walk with confidence on the way over, but I almost trip. A small gasp slips through my lips, and my heart stutters in my chest. Luckily, Lucian hooks me with his arm and keeps me from falling, smoothly guiding me to the table like nothing happened. My heart's in my throat as I walk the remaining few steps, my cheeks burning with embarrassment. I don't look around to see if anyone saw.

The waiter produces two menus but Lucian politely waves

him away as he says, "I already know what we'd like to order."

"Of course, sir." Another young man dressed in a crisp black suit quietly fills the crystal globe glasses on our table with water from a pitcher as Lucian orders.

"A bottle of chardonnay to drink, black cod brûlée," Lucian nods in my direction while passing the menus back, "and ribeye with goat cheese dipped in Meyer lemon honey mustard."

The waiter slips the menus back into a pouch at his waist, and takes out a pen and pad in one smooth flourish.

I part my lips to say something about Lucian ordering for me, but then close them. He's still my Dom. The rules have changed slightly, but not really.

"You'll love it," Lucian assures me with a small smile, seeing the question in my eyes.

"Of course, sir." The waiter nods as he scribbles notes on his pad. "Any appetizers?"

Lucian shakes his head. "No, thank you."

"I'll be back as soon as I can with your drinks. Please let me know if there's anything else I can do for you."

I watch as he walks away, past a few tables of romantic couples dining in luxury and try to relax in my seat. But my nerves have a grip on me. Blowing out a breath, I take a peek around and my stomach tightens even more. I can't get over the fact that I'm dining with the upper crust of society. Club X had filthy rich diners, but that's different. There, it's horny rich men looking to pay money to hook up with women from all socioeconomic backgrounds. Here, everyone's come to spend a boatload of money on food just because they can.

And I'm probably the only woman in the room who's here as almost a paid prostitute. The thought is unsettling and makes my stomach turn. I reach for my water, the crystal glass cold in my hand and take a sip.

I nervously finger my silverware, not sure how to act. I feel so anxious, I almost want to get up and leave. Why did Lucian bring me here again? Our contract said nothing about wining and dining with rich people. I thought it was all supposed to be about sex, whips and chains. Maybe this is some sort of test.

Noticing my nervousness, Lucian hooks his finger under my chin, drawing my eyes to him.

"You need to relax, treasure," he says softly. His eyes are filled with empathy and his concern goes a long way in calming my anxiety. "These people aren't any better than you are. Trust me on that." He says his words with such conviction that I actually believe him for a short moment.

Looking at him, I'm reminded again of his words in the car. *I respect your needs and your submission, and you do the same for me and my dominance. It's about trust, respect and communication.*

Before I can say anything in return, the waiter comes back, gently setting our wine glasses down in front of us one by one and pouring a small amount of the wine in Lucian's glass.

Lucian motions for him to continue pouring without taking a sip. "Is there anything else I can do for you?" the waiter asks as he finishes pouring the wine and then gently sets the bottle on the table.

"No," Lucian replies. "Thank you."

A moment passes in silence. Lucian grabs his glass of wine and relaxes in his seat. I envy him. He seems so at ease in this setting, so used to being surrounded by such awesome wealth.

"So how did you find out about Club X?" Lucian asks suddenly, looking at me with an intensity that makes me forget about all my worries for a moment and causes a shiver to run down my spine. Although I'm still slightly on edge, I love the way he's looking at me; like I'm the only one in the room. And seeing as how we're surrounded by beautiful, wealthy-looking women that make me feel insecure, I feel pretty fucking special right about now.

I pause for a moment, lowering my gaze, my skin pricking at the soft emotions swelling my breasts. I'm unsure if I should tell him how Carla approached me and swore me to secrecy, but I decide there's little harm. He's a member of Club X, not an outsider. I won't be revealing anything about the club he doesn't already know. "My friend, Carla, told me about it one day out of the blue," I say softly.

Lucian arches a brow, his fingers running along the stem of his glass. "Any particular reason?"

I blush slightly at the memory, but I'm glad that we're

talking. The conversation is helping me relax, and focusing on Lucian is making it easy to tune out the people around me. "She invited me because she said she could tell I'd like it. She said I was an obvious Submissive and that I'd enjoy it."

Lucian takes a sip of his chardonnay, still looking at me in a way that makes my skin prick. "So, you said your friend's name is Carla?"

"Yes," I reply. "Her Dom is named Bruce, and he's actually her boyfriend." Including that small bit of information makes my blood heat with insecurity. *She's more to him than I am to Lucian.* I have to look away from Lucian and clear my throat before continuing. "I don't know if you know him or not."

A thoughtful expression graces Lucian's handsome face. "Hmm. Can't say that I've heard of those two before, and I usually know who the couples are within the club." Lucian's eyes grow distant and I know he's thinking about some event in the past, something that troubles him because his demeanor has shifted. "But then again, I've been away from the club for a while."

I clear my throat and ask, "Will we be going back to the club anytime soon?"

"If you'd like, we can." He straightens in his seat and clears his throat, the hard lines on his face softening. "In fact, I've been meaning to talk to you about that."

"About what?" I ask curiously.

"I think it might be beneficial for you to be around other

couples, get used to how they interact. It'll help you with training."

I nervously half smile. I'm anxious about trying something outside my safe zone, and I prefer the privacy of Lucian's playroom, but I'm anxious to see more of the club. "I think so, too," I agree, a small thrill running through me.

Lucian seems pleased at my response and he once again gives me that look that makes my skin prick. "You're so beautiful, do you know that?"

I blush furiously, my heart doing backflips at his unabashed praise. That compliment was totally unexpected. Lucian's really making me feel like that we actually are a couple, even though this is supposed to be pretend. I have to shake my head and remind myself that this isn't real. It's all make-believe. "Thank you," I say in a soft voice, a shy smile on my lips.

Lucian shakes his head. "No thanks needed here. So why is it that you decided to enter the auction?"

I freeze as his question triggers those dark memories that are always waiting for the right moment to pounce. The very reasons that drove me to Club X. Several painful images flash in front of my face and I have to grip the edges of the table to keep my composure. I lower my gaze, breathing deeply, slowly, fighting to push those horrible images away. Not here. Not now. *Go the fuck away.*

When I look up, Lucian is staring at me with concern in

his eyes and my heart is suddenly aching for him. Maybe I should just be open with him. Doesn't he have the right to know? A powerful urge presses down on my chest, bidding me to tell him everything.

I respect your needs and your submission, and you do the same for me and my dominance. It's about trust, respect and communication.

His words bear heavy on my conscience. If I truly want our relationship and contract to be successful, shouldn't I be truthful with him and let him know who he's really dealing with? Isn't that what trust is all about?

"Treasure?" Lucian's deep voice snaps me to attention.

I open my mouth, ready to tell him everything, but no words come out. I can't bring myself to say it, can't bring myself to reveal my dark secret. A secret that could possibly push Lucian away. Fuck. I feel ashamed. I wish this wasn't so fucking awkward, too.

I give Lucian a light, fraudulent smile and shrug. "I don't know... I just... wanted to try it." I feel shitty for lying, and it's so fucking obvious that I am, but what else can I do? I'm not telling Lucian about my past. At least not right now. I don't want to mess up our arrangement in any way. It's just sex. And it's over in less than a month. I don't owe him anything more.

Lucian peers at me, his eyes piercing me with their skepticism. "Are you sure there isn't something else you aren't telling me?"

I almost fold beneath his questioning gaze, my heart hammering in my chest. It's funny how the tables turn. A minute ago I was prying into his past, but now he's prying into mine. *And he didn't open up to me.* The reminder hardens my resolve. I duck my head, tearing my eyes from his and look down into my glass of water. "I'm sure," I repeat firmly, injecting as much strength into my voice as possible to get him off my back.

It's about trust, respect and communication, his words scream in my head, making me feel even more like shit.

Lucian stares at me intently, looking like he wants to press the issue, but then he straightens, a smile curling the corner of his lips as he takes a sip of his chardonnay. I relax slightly, realizing he's letting me off the hook. *Thank God.* He's definitely not buying my lie, though, and for some reason he seems content on letting me get away with it. For now.

A feeling of relief flows through me when the waiter returns with our food balanced in each hand. My stomach quietly rumbles as the rich aroma fills my nostrils and he sets the plates down in front of us.

"Anything else, sir?" the waiter asks.

"No, thank you," Lucian's quick to reply.

"Enjoy," he says. And with a flash of a smile, the waiter's gone.

Grabbing my heavy fork, I take a bite of the tender meat dipped in sauce, and my eyes widen as the sweet tangy flavor fills my mouth. Damn. Lucian is right.

"This is delicious," I remark, waiting for Lucian's gaze to meet mine. "Thank you." I hope he knows how serious I am.

Lucian grins. "I knew you would like it," he says confidently.

"So how did you become the CEO of your company?" I ask after a few more delicious bites. Having read the article about his rise to success, I pretty much know what Lucian is going to say, but I'd like to hear him tell it. I figure now is a good time as ever to hopefully turn this date around and focus on something that will lighten the mood.

Lucian eyes me. "How did you know I was CEO? Much less own my own company?" There's a bit of humor in his voice. I'm sure he knows I cyberstalked him.

I freeze mid-bite, my mind racing with an explanation other than the obvious. *Fuck.* Lucian never told me what he did, and I never asked. Nor was there any mention of his occupation in the contract. I open my mouth to say, "I just assumed that," but then snap my lips shut, feeling a bite of shame. It's one thing to tell a lie because you're hiding something too personal to share, it's another to tell one to cover something harmless.

A blush reddening my cheeks, I sheepishly admit, "I looked you up on the net."

I brace myself, half expecting Lucian to go into a rage for my intrusion on his privacy, but he just chuckles. "I was sure you had, my sweet treasure," he says. "I'd do the same thing if I were in your shoes. Hell, it's the smart thing to do. I would never advise anyone to enter into a contract with a stranger without knowing something about them, especially someone you'd be entrusting with your safety."

I'm relieved that Lucian hasn't taken offense to my prying. For some reason, I keep waiting for him to punish me for any blunders. It's like the line is blurring between Dom Lucian and real Lucian. I don't know which one I'm talking to. "One thing the articles I read kept going on about was how young you were to head a successful startup," I add. "That's impressive."

Lucian nods. "I had some help from a friend. He's a silent partner now."

"What about your family?" I ask. "Did you come from," I wave my hand in the direction of the other guests, "this?" I don't know how to word it.

"No," Lucian says simply. "I'm from a blue collar family." The ease in his voice is gone, and I can tell I've struck a nerve. "They're dead to me now," he says quietly.

I sit there awkwardly, frustrated that we somehow keep making each other upset, but not quite knowing what to do. The anger in Lucian's voice... it's raw. There's pain there. And pain is an emotion I'm well accustomed to.

Moved by emotion and instinct, I swallow back a lump in my throat, and reach over and place my hand atop of his. His gaze drops to where our hands are joined, and my heartbeat slows. For an instant, I fear I've crossed the line. But he surprises me by giving me a glimpse of a smile and running his thumb gently over the back of my hand.

I tell him softly, my voice filled with empathy, my eyes finding his, "Sometimes family can do you worse than a person on the street would."

Trust me, I should know, I think to myself as those dark images threaten to come back. Nausea twists my stomach, and I'm angry at myself for even thinking about them right now.

My words seem to have a profound effect on Lucian because he visibly relaxes in his chair. "Thank you," he says warmly to me. He pauses and takes a deep breath, then lets out an explosive sigh. "And there's something else, too."

My heart jumps in my chest. Maybe he's about to reveal something. "What's that?"

"I was going through a divorce at the same time," he forces out.

I raise my eyebrows, surprised he would bring this up, but I'm hopeful that I'll find out what caused it and maybe find out what kind of man Lucian is.

Lucian nods, his eyes burning with anger and a hint of sadness. "It wasn't pleasant."

I lean forward slightly. "Did it have anything to do with..." I trail off, but I know he gets my meaning, though I feel like I'm once again walking on the edge by prying where I shouldn't. Yet, I can't help myself.

Lucian is quiet for a moment, digesting my question. Finally, he shakes his head. "No. My ex was into the same lifestyle, actually. We both enjoyed it." He huffs out a dry, humorless chuckle. "She craved the money more."

Damn. Why do I keep bringing these things up? "I don't know what to say," I say slowly.

"There's nothing for you to say," Lucian says dismissively. "I'm the one who's sorry."

"Well, I feel awful for even having brought it up. Sorry I asked."

Lucian waves my apology away again. "What's done is done." He looks at me, his eyes assessing me in a way that makes me feel fuzzy inside. "I'd rather focus on the here and now."

Unable to take his gaze, a blush comes to my cheeks and I lower my head.

"Look at me," Lucian commands.

I raise my eyes, my cheeks burning all the hotter. "Sir?" Crap. Why do I keep doing that?

"Lucian," he says firmly.

"Lucian," I repeat.

Fingering his wine glass, Lucian studies me, a slight smile on his lips and my skin pricks at the emotion that grips my chest. I recognize the feeling and it makes me nervous. Lucian said this was all for show, but why do I keep feeling like it's something more?

I need to just focus on the sex, I repeat to myself, *because that's all this is. For thirty days.*

"Would you like to go for a walk after dinner?" Lucian asks, his beautiful eyes still focused on me. "There's a cobblestone trail that leads to a bridge overlooking the water. On a night like this, I'm sure you'll love it." He pauses a moment, glancing at my blouse before adding, "I'll have a coat brought for you."

I pause, thinking, *No, what I want you to do is take me back to your place and make me beg for that big fat cock,* but I only feel more confused. I'm not sure what's to gain from taking a walk as a couple, if it's not supposed to be real. I thought he just wanted to show me off in public and then whisk me back away into privacy.

I part my lips, feeling an urge to decline. I'm already having trouble separating my sexual energy from my emotions and Lucian is sending me mixed signals, making it worse. But at the same time, I'm scared of angering him. He's a man that won't be denied, and I still feel like I'm his Sub, even out in public. "Yes," I reply dutifully, flashing a weak smile, my cheeks turning red yet again. "I would love that."

I don't miss the satisfaction that flashes in Lucian's eyes. "Good."

We continue eating our meal, our conversation turning to lighter things, and despite my nervousness, I find myself relaxing. Lucian's charm makes me feel at ease and he's showing a tender side of himself that I didn't think he possessed. Several times throughout the meal, I have to go back to reminding myself that he's just doing this for show and that he doesn't care one way or another about me, except for being his paid sex toy.

Still, I'm so charmed by his behavior, I find myself wondering if it would be better to just tell him the truth. Outside of the playroom, he seems like such a nice guy, and I feel guilty about lying even more now after hearing the story about his ex. Maybe disclosing the truth would improve my experience as his Sub instead of negatively impacting it.

If only I had the courage to find out.

Seeing my distressed expression, Lucian asks, "Something you want to tell me?"

Anxiety crushes my stomach as I look into Lucian's eyes. He's been so gracious to me tonight, even if it wasn't real, revealing things that he didn't have to share with me. But as much as I want to, I don't think I can bring myself to tell him. I feel like he wouldn't understand. How could he? Being a Dom is just a lifestyle to him, but being a Sub is a *need* for me.

Feeling sick to my stomach, I shake my head, plaster a fake smile on my face, and answer, "No... I was just thinking I didn't save room for dessert."

CHAPTER 17

LUCIAN

I lean back in my chair, facing the large window at the back of my office. From here, the skyline is quiet, moving slowly underneath me. Nothing at all like the reality of being on the busy streets of the city. From up here, it's calming. The steel and glass shine with a sleek beauty that radiates a sense of power.

I tap my thumb along the armrest of the chair, thinking about the other night. The phone on my desk rings and it draws my attention, but I hit the button to silence it. I don't need any interruptions right now. I rise from my seat and walk to the window. Last night was more enjoyable than I thought it would be. It was a success as well. Andrea and the agency are pleased with the article that'll be going live at some point today online and hitting the magazines tomorrow.

Most Eligible Bachelor is on the Dating Scene. ...how inaccurate. I sigh deeply and ignore the ill feelings stirring in the pit of my stomach. I'd rather stay away from the press altogether, but I've chosen this course of action. I'll see it through.

One thing I hadn't quite prepared was my reaction to taking my sweet treasure out. Her lack of understanding is drawing me in more than I ever thought it would. I'm actually excited to take her to the club tonight. I never thought I'd get the same thrill from Club X that I once had. But it's ringing in my blood.

There's something bothering her though. It was obvious with the way she was hesitating last night. I don't like it. I don't like her keeping secrets from me.

I've arranged for a private room tonight so I can get to the bottom of it. I'm sure a little orgasm denial will get her talking. Especially considering how disappointed she was last night before I took her out. An asymmetric grin kicks my lips up. She didn't fuss with her punishment though. She didn't argue with me. She's so fucking perfect, and she has absolutely no idea.

It's hard to believe she had no experience as a Sub before this. I remember our conversation about her ex, and the curiosity rises in me once again.

I walk back to my desk and click on the emails. Isaac should have a good bit of detail for me on Dahlia's last relationships. She's had social media profiles for years, so her background check and history will be sent to me shortly. Maybe I should feel ashamed for digging into her past and violating her privacy... but I don't. Not in the least. She's my Submissive, and therefore my responsibility.

Isaac's a professional. He's worked in security for years, and I can trust him. It's not the first time I've asked him to look into someone and he's done it with no questions asked.

My phone rings again, and I stare at it with irritation before finally lifting it off the hook and begrudgingly answering it.

"Stone."

"Mr. Stone, it's Andrea." I recognize her voice instantly. Andrea sounds less than her usual chipper self. She sounds nervous, and the realization makes me stand tall.

"Yes," I say in an even tone.

The sounds of her clearing her throat fill the phone as I wait with tense shoulders. Whatever it is, she can just spit it out. It better not have a damn thing to do with the article or my comment though. "My comment about Miss Days-"

"Mr. Stone, it's about your wife."

"*Ex*-wife." I'm quick to correct her. Unconsciously my ring finger twitches as I think about how a ring will never lay there again.

"I'm so sorry, sir. Your ex-wife. She's taking this to a different level now."

I huff a humorless laugh. "We took care of that problem,

didn't we?" With the photo and an agreement to several articles over the course of a month or so, the magazines are going for the hotter news and bigger paycheck.

I walk closer to the large window and look down at the tiny cars as they move slowly under me. Seemingly so slow. "She's decided that she's going to do a tell-all book now."

I grit my teeth, hating that she just won't let it go. What is it that she thinks is worth telling, exactly? A failed marriage because I worked too fucking much? I put a ring on the finger of a woman who was more interested in a paycheck than our relationship. I don't know how I let her fool me.

And as far as my perversions that she's willing to throw in my face, her tastes were far more extreme than my own. I take in a deep breath, trying to calm myself.

"What exactly is in this book?" I dare to ask.

"Mr. Stone," she says, then hesitates on the line. "According to the publisher who we've been in contact with," she hesitates again for a moment, "the book will have pictures of the aftermath of your sexual encounters."

My heart stills as she continues. *Pictures*? "There's no way for her to be able to verify that they were taken at the time of your marriage and I'm sure your lawyer will be able to prevent their use, but if this were to be leaked it would certainly be detrimental to your image."

"Pictures?"

"They make it appear as though there were bruises and

several abrasions." Her voice remains strong as she says, "The way it's written leaves a lot of implications. The editor and publisher have been in contact because of potential lawsuits."

Anger slowly rises in me as I close my eyes.

Never. I never leave marks, never leave cuts. Even when I picked up my first whip, I learned then the importance of only bringing the blood to the surface. Just enough force to redden the skin and create a wave of endorphins. I've never bruised anyone. Never. It's simply not my kink. She wants to paint herself as a victim. Probably even more so, she wants to paint me as a villain.

Andrea speaks before I'm able to respond.

"I'm certain these pictures are fabricated, Mr. Stone. Especially considering the toxicity of your divorce."

"You are correct," I answer her in a tight voice.

"They would have come up before, had there been any truth at all to what she's implying. The problem is that there's no way for us to prove this. The best possible line of defense would be for you to continue this relationship with your..." The rustling of paper in the background fills the silence.

"Dahlia." I say her name as I pinch the bridge of my nose.

"Yes, Miss Days."

"Is she saying I beat her?" I have to ask. "She's claiming abuse?" Even after everything we went through, I never thought she'd stoop so low. I *loved* her. I loved the woman I thought she was.

I'd never do anything to hurt her. Not like that. She loved the paddle, but it was only for play, only to intensify her pleasure. There was never a bruise on her body.

"She is." The truth slams against my chest as I lean against the window, the cool glass on my palms. "The wording is ambiguous, so you'll have to speak with Mr. Harris on that matter." Her voice is soft and laced with sympathy.

I clear my throat and reply, "I understand. Thank you, Andrea."

"I'm sorry, Mr. Stone." The words hang stale in the air as I tell her goodbye and listen to the soft click on the other end.

I hold the phone in my hand, long after the line has gone dead. I can't believe I was ever fooled by that woman. I loved her. I know I did, and I was so fucking wrong about her and everything.

I push away from the window at the sound of a knock on my door.

"Come in," I call out, setting the phone back down where it belongs.

"Mr. Stone," Linda enters with a mug of coffee in one hand and a stack of papers in the other. She walks briskly to my desk, setting them each down before smoothing her skirt while looking up at me with a smile.

It instantly vanishes when she sees my expression. "Is everything alright?" she asks.

I give her a tight smile and ignore the concern in her voice.

"Fine." I sift through the stack and recognize the contracts that are due today. "I'll sign these after lunch." It's nothing that can't wait.

Linda stands there for a moment and I can see she wants to pry, but she presses her lips into a thin line and nods her head. "You'll let me know if you need anything?" she asks.

"Of course." She leaves silently and the phone rings again. There are emails and meetings, contracts and press conferences. I don't feel like doing any of them.

I know exactly what I do want though. I silence the phone and grab my cell phone from the desk.

Dahlia's number is right there from when she called last night.

She didn't stay over last night. I had a four a.m. meeting with a company in Singapore. But she called when she got back to her place. Just like I told her to.

She's not perfect, but she's the perfect Submissive for me. She gives it her best effort. The training is the best part, and of course I always give her what she needs after she's thanked me for her punishment. I got very lucky with her.

I press send and listen to the phone ring... and ring.

She doesn't have work or classes today. I almost brought her into the office, but decided against it so that I could focus. But I need her now.

Of course she's not fucking answering the phone.

I call again rather than leaving a message, and again it

goes to voicemail.

Today has been a very trying day and I don't want to take it out on my sweet Submissive. I take in a deep breath, running my hands through my hair.

She's just busy for the moment. My desk phone rings as I breathe out and I glare at it. Hating the constant reminder that I'm stuck here instead of being with her. I'm tense and on edge. Close to ripping this fucking office apart.

I could do what I've done for the past three years. I could go to my gym and take my aggression out there. But I want to fuck. I want the exertion. I *need* the release.

I want to unwind and get lost in the feel of her tempting body.

You need to answer when I call you.

I press send on the text and sit in my seat, ignoring yet another phone call. I have actual work to do and I pay my lawyer and the agency enough money to take care of these problems for me. I should just let it roll off my shoulders and get this contract completed, but now I'm fixated on my treasure.

I go through at least a dozen emails, all with only partial focus. I keep thinking about Dahlia. Wondering what she's doing. I should know. I own her right now. My eyes dart from the screen to my phone.

Ten minutes later, and still nothing.

I expect you to be available for me at all times.

I send the text, feeling the anger rise higher.

She knows this. Dahlia's a smart woman. She's intelligent and knows the rules of this relationship. She's never been a Submissive, but she knows enough.

And I fucking paid for her. If I wanted I could have her at my feet right now, sucking me off. My dick instantly hardens with need at the thought. That's exactly what *should* be happening right now.

I understand she's busy, and that she wasn't expecting me. I hold on to the last thought. I can be reasonable. My expectations weren't made clear, and I assumed too much. She should know to wait for my call. But I haven't explicitly told her.

Anger simmers on the surface; I paid for her. Her time is mine, and I've been generous. Maybe too generous.

This is my fault, but when I get my hands on her, I'll make sure this never happens again.

CHAPTER 18

DAHLIA

*Y*ou *need to answer when I call you.*

I pull at the hem of my blouse with worry as I sit in the back seat of Lucian's Rolls Royce, reading his last text to me. I've texted him back several times, but he hasn't responded since he told me to wait for the car. I bite my lower lip, upset that I missed his calls and disappointed him. Worry stirs in the pit of my stomach as I meet Joseph's eyes in the rearview mirror.

I was at the mall shopping when he sent the texts and calls, busying myself with a gift for him, and my phone was at the bottom of my purse. I simply didn't hear it.

Everything is going to be okay, I tell myself, trying not to worry. *Lucian will understand.*

I glance down at the small bag at my side, my gift to

Lucian. I got him a coffee mug from a gift shop. He drinks it non stop. It's the first thing he gets in the morning. The words emblazoned on the side say, "Please, sir." When I bought it, I thought it was funny. Now I think it's stupid as hell. It's been fifteen days but it feels like so much longer.

I just wanted to get him something to say thank you. Lucian has been positively spoiling me over the last two weeks, sending boxes and boxes of expensive clothes, high heels, designer purses and seductive fragrances to my apartment door.

I'm still in shock over how much he's splurging on me, especially after buying my contract for so much. The cost of these gifts has to number in the thousands, and they're the nicest things anyone has ever bought me. It's hard not to think that Lucian cares about me since he's going to all this trouble. I just wanted to do something nice for him in return. I feel like there's something between us. Or there was. Now I'm just filled with worry.

I could be fooling myself though. Lucian's a billionaire. Money probably means nothing to him. A few thousand bucks to spend on his fuck toy that he'll discard within a few days probably doesn't make him bat a single eyelash.

My lips part into a soft sigh and my heart does a flip as I look out of the window and see Lucian. He looks hot as fuck, casually leaned back against the club's back wall, wearing black silk slacks and a white shirt that's unbuttoned at the collar, showcasing his tanned skin beneath, his hands stuffed in his pockets. He's wearing the same black mask he had on when I first met him, his eyes gazing at me through it with that intensity that makes me shiver.

As the car comes to a stop, he pushes off the wall and opens the door before Joseph can get out. "You've kept me waiting." There's a slight edge in his voice that causes my skin to prickle.

I grip my gift bag, intent on offering it to Lucian as a peace offering, and begin to open my mouth to say sorry, when Lucian gestures sharply and says, "Leave it. You won't be needing that."

"But it's a gift for you-" I begin to protest.

"Put it away," Lucian growls dangerously, stepping away from the wall and moving toward me. "Let Joseph take it away with him. You can retrieve it later."

I lower my head with shame at how close I'd come to arguing with my Dom. My heart beats faster, and anxiety swirls in my lower belly. Shit. "Yes, sir." Joseph appears at my side to take the gift bag from me as I get out of the car and stand by Lucian. Shivering with apprehension, I watch as he starts the engine and rolls off, leaving us alone.

I turn when I hear a step at my side and I look up into Lucian's mask, seeing only his piercing eyes. I let out a gasp and jump a little when he grabs me by the hips firmly, his touch sending sparks of electricity along my skin, pulling me into him. My breathing turns into soft pants as my core heats from being so close to his hard body. Below, I can feel his huge cock pressing against my stomach, pulsing with powerful need.

"I-I-I'm sorry," I stutter, unable to think clearly under his penetrating gaze, "about not seeing your text. I was shopping and my phone was at the bottom of my bag on vibrate." I cringe at how pathetic I sound, waiting for some type of punishment from Lucian, but he doesn't say anything and the corner of his lips curl up into a hint of a smile.

"Come," is all he says, pulling me along to a door in the private side entrance where two men in black suits and sunglasses stand guard. He makes a gesture at the two men, some sign that I can't quite make out, and they nod and open the door for us.

I follow Lucian as he drags me inside to a dark hallway with dim lighting. The lighting is so low that I can't really see, and I have to hold onto Lucian to make sure I don't bump into anything. We round a corner and the low lighting changes to a dark red. I look around, trying to get my bearings, but all I see are multiple doors up and down the hall. I don't know where Lucian's taking me; I've never been in this part of the club before.

At the end of the hallway are two large double doors. Lucian stops us in front of them and quickly punches in a code on a metal box mounted on the side panel. I hear a clicking sound and the doors swing open. My breath catches in my throat as I step into a room awash with grey and white.

In the center of the room sits an elegant bed with a canopy, its lush comforter matching the colors of the room, and at the foot of the bed is a plush grey couch. The walls seem to be lined with a grey velvet fabric, and the curtains are a creamy white. Several elegant desks are placed on either side of the room and there is a large china cabinet filled with sexual toys and devices.

This must be one of the private rooms, I think to myself as I hear the doors slam shut behind me. *Elegant and high class, but still equipped with the right stuff.*

Before I can take in everything, I'm roughly jerked into Lucian's arms from behind. I tremble against his hard body, my mind racing with anticipation of what's to come, feeling his huge hard dick pressing up against my ass and his breath hot on my neck.

"Sorry isn't good enough, treasure," he growls in my ear, causing my pussy to clench with insatiable need.

"Sir," I whimper softly not knowing what to say, aching to have his cock thrusting inside of my swollen pussy. I want him to punish me for my crime, ravaging my pussy with his big hard dick while spanking my ass like I've stolen something. God. I fucking crave it.

I cry out as he grips my blouse and lets out a bestial grunt, practically tearing it apart with his bare hands and then moving on to my bra, skirt and panties until I stand before him completely naked, trembling with need. My nipples pebble as the cool air hits them, and goosebumps rise on my flesh.

Without giving me time to react, Lucian drags me toward the bed and throws me on top of it. I land on the plush mattress with a bounce, my head slamming into the pillows. Before I can move, Lucian's on top of me, turning me onto my stomach, his hard dick throbbing against my ass, tying my hands and feet with grey cloth that he's pulled off the canopy. I tremble with my breath caught in my throat as he works, bucking slightly against him, but he's too strong. When he's done, I struggle against my binds, but they're tied so tight. He has me securely locked down.

I lie there helplessly, my breathing coming in short pants and look to the side and see him grab a blindfold that's sitting on the nightstand next to the bed. He stands over me with it, almost as if he's taunting me with what's to come. I strain my neck to look up at him, and the only thing I can see are those beautiful eyes of his flashing with something dark, and I plead, "Please, sir."

Lucian responds by placing the blindfold over my eyes, eliminating my sight.

"I had to wait for you," I hear him growl somewhere nearby, "now you will fucking wait for me." I listen as I hear him walk away, his footsteps receding until all I hear is... silence.

I lie still for him for what feels like forever, and the only sound I hear is my own breathing. I accept my punishment. It's not the first time he's punished me. But this is different. This is more intense. I shiver repeatedly as a cool draft touches my skin, again and again, and I know my entire body is covered in goosebumps.

Thump! I jump at the sound of what sounded like a very deliberate footstep, my heart bucking in my throat, and then I hear another heavy footstep followed by another and another. My breathing quickens in relief and part anxiety. Lucian's back.

I go completely still, knowing that's what he wants, knowing it's the only thing that will get me what I so badly crave.

I nearly buck as I feel something hard graze my skin, leaving goosebumps down my thigh, before it's pulled back. A soft moan escapes my lips as my core heats with desire. This is it. This is what I've been waiting for. It's what I fucking deserve.

"Not only have you left me waiting, but you lied to me, treasure," I hear Lucian say quietly from behind me. The quiet before the storm.

Smack!

I gasp with pain and pleasure, grabbing my binds to bear it, my pussy clenching violently around nothing. Immediately after, I feel Lucian kneading my ass, calming the pain pulsing through my ass cheeks.

"Tell me why you lied to me, treasure," I hear him whisper near my ear, his breath hot on my neck.

Shock goes through me, mixed with desire. Lied? What did I lie about?

"I know you've been hiding something. And you need to tell me what it is." Lucian's voice is hard. "You should have already told me."

Lucian knows? My heart races with anxiety. He knows what I'm hiding from him? I almost shake my head. That doesn't make sense. He can't know. I haven't told him anything.

But that doesn't mean he can't guess, a voice inside my head says, *he's not stupid.*

I part my lips to deny his words, and claim I don't have any idea what he's talking about, but guilt presses down upon my chest, keeping me from saying it. I don't know why I keep fighting to hold my secret. I'm tired of holding it in. I should just let it out and let the chips fall where they may.

"I'm sorry," I whimper, a soft admission.

Smack!

My body jolts violently and a strangled cry rips from my lips, my pussy moist with arousal.

"That's not what I asked for, treasure," I hear Lucian say somewhere through my mire of pain. His voice sounds like he's daring me to try to lie to him. And I wonder again why I'm fighting. It feels like he's already won.

I writhe on the bed from the sting of the savage blow he dealt against my ass, my mind a mix of pain, pleasure and confusion. I wait for another blow, but it isn't forthcoming. He's allowing me a moment of recovery, a moment to reflect on his words.

Tell him, my mind screams. *Tell him and let this all be over with!*

Smack! Smack!

Fuck! Tears leak from the corners of my eyes. This is different from the other punishments. There's no pleasure. Red is on the tip of my tongue. But a part of me knows I deserve this. That I *need* this.

Smack!

I suck in a sharp, painful breath, parting my lips to tell him what he wants to hear. *That I'm broken.*

Smack!

The strangled scream that escapes my lips is raw and filled with pain, but I manage to get three words out.

"I'll tell you!"

CHAPTER 19

LUCIAN

The last few hours have been difficult. When the emails came through and Isaac called, I couldn't believe what he'd told me. I saw the records, the charges against her father's brother. Isaac had a timeline of how her life fell apart, the court dates and her parents' divorce. Moving from one house to the next.

I knew she was hiding something. I never expected that though. Never.

How could she not tell me?

I'm crushed by the feeling of insignificance. I feel useless. Or at least to her I was. She didn't tell me because she didn't think I'd make a difference. Isaac's still looking into her ex, but I have no clue if she told him, or anyone else before him. Maybe she wants to keep it a secret. Maybe it wasn't mine to know.

But she's mine. My body heats with guilt for taking her the way I did. I assumed. No, I trusted she was forthcoming. She's my Submissive, and I had no idea about something so crucial to her needs. I still don't know everything. I don't know how this affects what she needs.

I'm going to find out though.

"It's alright, treasure," I whisper softly, cupping her face in my hand and kissing her tears away as I release the cuff from around her wrist. "It took a lot for you to tell me; I'm proud of you."

My voice is soft and comforting as I massage her arm and then release the other wrist. Her eyes are glassed over with tears and shining with insecurity.

"I'm sorry," her voice cracks as she wipes under her eyes.

She has nothing to be sorry about though, this is my fault. It was my responsibility, but I was too eager and too presumptuous.

I grip her hip and pull her closer to me. "Relax, Dahlia," I whisper into her hair as she leans against my chest. "I need you to talk to me, Dahlia."

I hold her close, running my hand down her back in soothing strokes. I knew she was hiding something from me. I could see that she so badly wanted to confide in me, but she didn't.

What I don't know is why. Why hide it? Did she think it was truly unnecessary, and that her past has no bearing on our current relationship? That's possible, and I was hopeful. But her current state begs to differ.

"Tell me, treasure," I say and gently press my lips to her forehead. My words fall into the space between us, "Tell me why you kept this from me."

She stills in my arms. I don't want to push her. Trust takes time, but I want this from her. I need this, or I won't be able to continue the way we were.

I need to know what I'm doing isn't hurting her.

"It doesn't matter."

Her words are hollow and soft. Her voice is chilled with the sadness that's echoed in her body language as she tries to push me away.

I let her. She's not going anywhere. She's stuck in this room with me and she can turn away from me and hide for the moment like she's been doing, but she's not leaving.

She doesn't have to tell me just yet. But I'm not going to let her lie. Not to me, and not to herself.

"It does matter," I say and brace my arm around her body, caging her in slightly and refusing to let her move away any farther. "You don't have to tell me any more than you want, but whatever comes out of your mouth needs to be the truth."

Dahlia hides her face from me, burying herself into the mattress. I'll allow it for a moment. I forced her to open up to me, but I can only push her so much. If she keeps running, it'll force me to break her. She can't hide from me. I won't allow it. Not when it comes to this.

"You aren't broken."

Her eyes whip to mine. Red-rimmed and her cheeks tearstained, even in such distress she looks beautiful. Maybe even more so because of it. "I am," she says and her voice is hard. "I can't..." her voice croaks, and she trails off. "I can't get off..."

Bullshit. I know she's cum for me. I hold in a breath and wait for more.

Her head hangs low and she picks at the comforter, her voice soft as she admits, "I have to feel like I'm being forced."

I keep my expression neutral, but internally I'm breaking, going over every encounter we've had. I can't remember one time where I wasn't rough with her. I knew she enjoyed it, but I didn't consider why. It's a simple preference for me. And I made the assumption that it was for her as well.

I set my hand down on her hip and scoot her a bit closer to me. As I think of what to say, I remember being gentle with her, early in the morning at the end of our first week. She was sore, and I didn't want to hurt her.

I suck in a breath, hating that I have to ask, but already knowing the answer.

"You've only cum for me when I was harsh with you?" She tenses under my embrace, but I continue to hold her.

"Yes," she softly whispers.

I feel sick knowing, hearing her confession. I took

pleasure and failed her as a Dom.

"I'm sorry, treasure, I didn't know."

I fell asleep holding her, after causing *that*. Leaving her unsatisfied, but even worse, with a trigger of what happened to her. Completely unaware. I know I'm a selfish man, but I've never felt it quite like I do in this moment.

"It's fine," she says, once again refuting the truth.

"It's not fine," I whisper, shaking my head gently. She doesn't hold my gaze, and her shoulders hunch forward. That never should have happened.

I consider my next words carefully. "Are you happy with not being able to find your release any other way?" I ask her. However she chooses to cope is just that, her choice. But this wouldn't be upsetting her so much if she was happy. I just need to hear her say it.

She shakes her head and looks up at me with pure vulnerability in her eyes. Tears fall down her cheeks. "No, no, I don't want this." I pull her soft body into my chest and hold her while she cries harder than before.

"Have you talked to anyone about this?"

"I have a therapist," she says, wiping under her eyes. I lean across the bed and grab a few tissues for her. She takes them graciously, whispering, "Thank you."

I nod my head. I think a therapist is far better equipped than I am. I'm out of my realm of expertise. I know I can help her. I can train her to find her release. I know I can give her that. I can show her she's capable.

"I'm sorry," she apologizes again, and I don't like it. I don't need her to tell me she's sorry. I need her to tell me she wants me to help. That she believes I can help her.

"Don't be. I'm here for you."

"I can give you what you need," I say quietly.

She nods her head, but she's not really understanding.

"I'm going to show you how deserving you are." Her sad expression stares back at me, she's exhausted and emotional.

And I'm sure she's hungry. One need at a time. I'll take care of her.

"Come, treasure. I need you to clean yourself up for dinner." She sniffles and nods her head, but before she can move off the bed, I wrap my arm around her waist and bring her closer to me.

"First, tell me something."

"What?" she asks warily.

"Anything," I tell her. I just want her to talk to me.

"Anything?"

I nod my head and repeat, "Anything," and kiss the tip of her nose. She smiles and curls up slightly, leaning next to me and looking across the room.

"I like lemon flavored Italian water ice the best."

A small laugh leaves my lips in a huff. "Lemon?" I say with a smile.

She looks up at me, expectantly. It takes me a moment

to realize what she's waiting for. "Cherry. I think I prefer cherry."

"You need to have your bracelet on," I tell her, grabbing her wrist and slipping the triple-ringed bracelet on before we can leave. Security knew she was coming while I waited for her. But I don't want to piss them off parading her around without the required membership bracelet. I hold her waist as we walk to the door. She's much better now that I've given her time to get ready. She needs touch though. She's still hurting. I can see it in her eyes.

I lead her out of the room, my hand along her back and it's only then that I realize she's not collared. I can't allow that. I want everyone to know she's mine.

"To the right, treasure," I say and pull her slightly, my fingers slipping around her waist, my thumb brushing easily along her hip and bringing her closer to me as we enter the Club X store, Sex and Submission.

"You need a collar." She smiles slightly and looks up at me as the words hit her. That touch of shyness comes over her as she brushes her hair behind her ear. I love that about her. That sweet bashfulness that she has.

I should have already bought her a collar. From the moment she set foot through those doors, she should have been labeled as mine. I'll have to get her a necklace, too. I always want a symbol of my possession around her neck.

The shop's walls are made of glass and arranged in a way that makes it look as though it's all purposefully arranged decoration. Just like the rest of the club, it shines with luxury.

Dahlia's eyes lock onto the collars on black velvet display stands the moment we enter. There are a variety, but none of them are good enough. She should be draped in gold. Just as she was when I first saw her. I'll get her something temporary for now, but as soon as we're home, I'm buying her one that's deserving of her beauty.

Dahlia walks toward the collars of her own accord and then freezes, looking back at me with frightened eyes. I merely nod and stay by the register.

She gently touches a few collars, but doesn't pick any of them up although she goes back to one three times before she finally settles on it.

It's a simple flat silver band with a single loop at the front, and a lock and key closure.

Knowing she won't be able to take it off once I put it on her sends a thrill I can only partially understand shooting through me.

I'm more than happy she chose one with this type of closure, and I make a mental note to make sure her next collar has the same. I glance at the price tag on the underside before making my way to the register. $15,000. Dahlia seems somewhat uncomfortable behind me, a question on the tip of her tongue, but she doesn't ask it.

"Member ID?" the woman behind the counter asks softly as I pass her the collar.

"Mister 646D," I answer. I could use my name, but I still prefer the anonymity.

"And would you like it now, or shall I box it for you?"

"I'll have it now." I quickly take it, along with the lock and turn to my treasure. She lifts her thick locks up and shivers as I slip the metal collar around her neck. I'm tempted to put the lock in the front, so everyone can see, but I place it on her as it's meant to go and run my hands down her shoulders and kiss her hair before slipping the lock into my pocket.

"All set?" I ask the attendant. They charge my tab rather than requiring cards to be used. It's more convenient this way.

"Yes, sir. I hope you two have a delightful evening."

I can't help but glance at the collar around my treasure's neck as we leave. Her fingers gently touch the silver band.

"Do you like it?" she asks me as we walk through the hallway and to the restaurant for dinner.

"I love it, because it shows them all that you belong to me." Her lips part with a lust-filled gasp, and she reaches for my hand. Before she can pull it away, like she's done so many times before, I snatch it and give her a gentle squeeze before bringing her hand to my lips and kissing the underside of her wrist.

The hallway is empty, and the faint sounds from the

playroom diminish the closer we get to the dining hall. Dahlia looks back twice at the sounds of a whip and then again at the sounds of a loud moan.

Her innocence pulls a smirk to my lips.

I nod at Isaac, the first person I see as we walk through the grand entrance and make my way over to him, proudly leading Dahlia toward him. I watch as he takes her in. She's not dressed as she should be. But she wasn't prepared, and I have no intention of taking her to the playroom now. Just dinner, and then home. We'll come back for a show and she can get a taste of what the club has to offer. But only once I know how to help her better. I need to make sure every action aids in her recovery.

Isaac tips his beer at me as we take a seat in his booth. It's in the back of the hall and facing the stage with a good view of everyone else. Working security, he's always chosen seats with ample viewing and easy access to an exit. Some things never change.

Dahlia's quiet as we take our seats and she's so tense, it seems she's not even breathing. "Relax, treasure," I whisper into her ear and gently kiss her cheek.

"How are you enjoying Lucian's company, Dahlia?" Isaac asks, and her eyes widen for a split second, wondering how he knew her name. I have no intention of telling her, so she can continue to wonder.

"I'm..." she pauses, considering her words. "It's better

than I ever hoped it would be." There's clear sincerity in her voice, and it fills my chest with a warmth I haven't felt in quite some time. Pride runs through me.

"She's a natural," I say as I gently brush her hair, watching a soft blush rise to her cheeks.

"You got lucky," Isaac says, tipping his beer at me.

"Where's-" Dahlia starts to ask, but then closes her mouth and stares down at the table.

"Where's?" he asks her with a raised brow. She's slow to reach his gaze, and I place my hand on her back.

"You were engaged in conversation, treasure. You can speak your mind."

Isaac's brow furrows as he says, "He's been keeping you sheltered." He takes another swig and then leans across the table, closer to Dahlia. "He's been selfish not to bring you around." A small huff of a laugh leaves Dahlia's lips, and she smiles slightly.

My shoulders tense slightly at the accusation, not because I'm jealous of Isaac, not because the humor is lost on me, but because it's true.

I don't want to be here. I don't want to have to wear a mask. I don't want to hide, and at the same time, I don't want to be watched. I don't trust people. I haven't in years. Most notably because of Tricia.

We came here weekly when we were married. We were known to be a pair. And when our marriage crumbled, I'm ashamed to admit, I was embarrassed to come back.

It took time, and I finally gave it another chance. But it's not the same. I don't feel... welcomed. It's as though they're watching and sizing me up. Wondering why my Submissive left me. Wondering how I failed.

My own insecurities have kept me from bringing my sweet treasure here. But I'm willing to offer her this. I think it will help her. Not only to learn how a true Submissive and Dominant interact, but also to watch various erotic encounters. She needs the experience. I know it will help her.

"Where's your Submissive?" Dahlia asks Isaac as a waitress brings the menus and sets them in front of each of us. The easiness from the other night is finally starting to creep back into Dahlia's demeanor. Dahlia doesn't move to take hers. Good girl. I want to pick for her. I want something divine for her tonight.

"Could I get you anything to drink, sirs?" the waitress asks.

"A whiskey on the rocks for me," I answer easily. The waitress nods her head and then looks back to Isaac.

"I think just a water for now," he says. Club X has a three-drink maximum. Any more and you aren't able to enter the club. Only the dining hall.

"What's your favorite drink?" I lean down and ask Dahlia. The waitress is waiting, and I know she won't write anything down until I agree to whatever it is that Dahlia says.

"My favorite?" she asks, and then hums as she thinks of

her answer. "A margarita, but I don't-"

Isaac laughs in his seat, interrupting her and I take the opportunity to tell the waitress, "A margarita, please."

"Frozen, or on ice?" she asks.

I look to my Submissive and she answers the waitress, "Frozen, with salt, please."

"Salt?" Isaac asks, "Is there any other way?"

"Some of my friends like sugar." Isaac makes a face that mirrors my distaste.

"So?" Dahlia looks at Isaac, "your Submissive?"

"I haven't got one," Isaac says with a smile that's plastered on. It's not meant to be there. Isaac has been soft lately. Ever since his last Submissive. He's been unwilling to take another.

"Oh, are you going to..." Dahlia stops talking as we both watch her, waiting for what's next. In my time with her, she's seemed so confident and poised. But she's not in this atmosphere. I need to fix that. Yet one more instance in which I've failed her.

"Buy one?" he asks.

Dahlia nods her head. "Yes, at auction?"

Isaac frowns and shakes his head. "I doubt it. I'm just enjoying the company and helping where I can."

I grunt a laugh. He doesn't want the responsibility anymore. He's missing out, and he knows it. But I can't blame him when I did the same thing.

At least I didn't come here though.

"Oh, how do you help?" Dahlia asks with genuine curiosity.

"Shows and demonstrations."

"Isaac is an expert with the whip." Dahlia shifts slightly at my mention of the whip. And it forces a smirk to my lips.

As the waitress comes and gently sets our drinks down one at a time from a large silver tray, Dahlia's phone rings. Her eyes dart to mine, and I nod slightly.

"I'm sorry."

"Nothing to be sorry for. If I didn't want your phone on, I would have made that clear." I lean closer to her, cupping her chin in my hand. "I think you should be in the habit of listening for your phone though, my sweet treasure." Her face brightens with a beautiful pink as I quickly kiss her lips and release her.

The uneasiness of the day settles against my chest as I lift my whiskey to my lips, the scent filling my lungs. I throw it back, knowing she's not alright. *We* aren't alright. This isn't an easy fix, and I'm going to have to be slow and patient. Two things I've never been very good at.

I lock eyes with Isaac as Dahlia busies herself looking in her purse. Isaac's worked in security for so long and dealt with a number of victims. I'm sure he has an opinion of my sweet treasure. He's a good man, and he hated to tell me what happened to her. I haven't talked to him since earlier, and I can see the questions in his eyes.

I give him an imperceptible nod. I know she's going to be alright. I'll make damn sure of it.

His shoulders relax slightly, and his relief is evident. I wrap my arm around Dahlia's shoulders, consumed by the need to touch her and protect her, my desire just to have her close.

A soft noise from behind us gains Isaac's attention.

"I'll be right back," he says with his eyes on the sweet little thing who just walked into the room, her hand gently settling on the bannister, bracing herself. Her eyes are large and full of shock and wonder. There's no collar around her neck and she's walking aimlessly in the room, searching for where she belongs. Her short jumper looks out of place, further making her stand apart from the crowd. But what captures my attention are the thin silver scars on her back. So thin, they wouldn't be visible if not for the exact placement of the sconces in the dining hall.

I watch as Isaac approaches her and she falls slowly to the floor, never looking him in the eyes. It's obvious she's been trained before. But not by anyone here.

"It's all so overwhelming," Dahlia's soft voice brings me back to her. My sweet treasure. She doesn't belong here, but not because she doesn't fit in. She does, so well. She doesn't belong here because she should be home with me. Healing and working on feeling whole. I hate that I ever acted in a way that contributed to her pain.

No matter what she says, I did.

I took her in a way that resulted in her being in pain. It's unacceptable. I need to make this right. But there are only weeks left.

I need more time.

"You're coming back with me, and I want you to stay with me." I say the words as a command although it toes the line of the freedom I've given her thus far into the contract. I can see her protests in her eyes, although she remains quiet. She's thinking that I think less of her. That I think she's broken. *That I pity her.* But I don't. She's strong and capable, just like she was yesterday. But I can offer her solace. And I want to. I desperately crave to fill those needs that she's ignored.

"I'm your Dom. I need to fix this so you can better serve me." It's easy to make it sound selfish. I am a selfish man. And I'm pushing her. But that's what I'm supposed to do. My role is to push her to her limits. She can handle this. She's strong enough.

She hesitates and looks around the dining hall, as if only now realizing where we are. Her beautiful eyes raise to meet mine and she softly agrees, "Yes, sir."

CHAPTER 20

DAHLIA

I*'m your Dom. I need to fix this so you can better serve me.*

Sitting at my desk at work, I mindlessly finger the necklace, a gift from Lucian, at my throat. I have emails piling up that I need to respond to, but I can't get my mind off my current dilemma; I think I'm falling for Lucian. I know I shouldn't be, given our complicated pasts, but I feel like he's the first person to ever truly understand me. I'm still in shock that he didn't call off our contract after learning my secret. Or that he didn't shy away from my claims of being broken. It seemed to only make him *more* determined to help me.

I can't believe that he's willing to take on my emotional baggage when he can just walk away and find himself another Sub who doesn't have the same hang-ups. He doesn't have to waste his time with me, he can have any woman he wants. But it shows that he cares. And I want his help. I *need* his help. Even if it makes me seem weak. I don't care.

Still, I'm worried that I'm setting myself up for disappointment. I can feel myself being weak for him. I'm relying on him, and that's something I don't do. I feel there's a good chance Lucian won't be able to help me and I'll end up with an aching heart. To add to my insecurities, last night definitely gave me doubts about our future.

I suck in a heavy breath at the memory.

I'd tried to give Lucian a blowjob when it was time for bed, but he claimed he was tired and needed to sleep. He gently brushed my hair away from my face and told me to lie down. I did as I was told, but I hated it. I wanted to accept him at his word, but I couldn't stop thinking he just didn't want me because of my problem. Because *I'm broken.* It took a lot for me to hold myself together and my self-esteem took a blow. I started to think I wasn't good enough. That *he* thought I wasn't good enough for him. And that he's only trying to help me because he pities me.

I can only hope that it's all in my head.

Breaking out of my dark thoughts, I let out a soft sigh of frustration as I look at the tons of emails on my computer screen. *I'm never gonna get any work done.*

Trying to push my situation from my mind, I begin to go about answering emails, starting with the most important ones first. By midday I'm halfway through my workload and I've taken a break to type a message to my therapist when Carla nearly breaks her neck bursting into my office. She's holding a newspaper clutched to her chest, her expression animated and excited. As usual, she's dressed stylishly today in a black pantsuit and cream camisole peeking out from underneath, her hair pulled back into a single braid, bangs covering her forehead, rosy rouge coloring her cheeks and purple shadow frosting her eyelids.

She shakes the paper at me, her chest heaving violently, making me think she's sprinted all the way up to my office without pausing to take a breath. "You will not believe what's on the front page of the Daily Observer!" she gasps.

My curiosity piqued, I quickly close out the email that I was typing to my therapist about making an appointment so that Carla doesn't see. I don't need her thinking I'm broken, too.

"What's that?" I ask, standing up to take the paper from Carla. I'm trying to be my normal self, but I just don't have the peppy outlook I usually do. I'm tired, and my spirits are dampened.

"Just look at it!" wheezes Carla.

I snatch the paper from her hands and flip it around to the first page. A jolt of shock runs through me as my gaze settles on the page and I let out a soft gasp, my eyes going wide. The headline in bold takes my breath away.

Hot, Eligible CEO Bachelor's new fling!

It's a picture of me and Lucian on the night we had dinner at the restaurant, embracing and engaged in a heated kiss. Lucian's hand is on my ass, and my arms are wrapped around my neck. My heart pounds. I know right when it was taken. I remember that moment like it happened only a minute ago.

"Crazy, huh?" Carla breathes next to my ear as she looks at the picture with me, causing me to jump. I was so engrossed with the picture that I forgot that she was even there. "Where the hell were you two at?"

I'm unable to respond, my eyes glued to the picture. A surge of powerful emotion runs through me. I can't get over how much we look like a couple. Even though it was all supposed to be for show it almost looks... real. Like we really are in love.

My heart does a flip at the thought and I go weak in the knees, confirming what I felt earlier; I'm falling for Lucian. It scares the hell out of me. This, what we have, is fragile. It all hinges upon the fact he wants to *fix* me. But what happens when he decides I'm not worth the trouble? Or when my contract is up in nine days? My lips draw down into a frown as emotion threatens to overwhelm me.

And what will Lucian think about this? My blood spikes with anxiety. I can't even begin to think of his reaction. I try to swallow, but it feels like my heart is shoved up my throat and trying to get away from me.

Carla stares at me, noticing my conflicted expression. "What's wrong?" she asks me, placing her hand on my arm with concern. "Why aren't you happy?"

I set the paper down on my desk and turn to her, parting my lips to say something, but then feel a lump the size of a golf ball fill my throat, staying my words. I don't know what's wrong with me. I just want this to be as real as this picture looks. I want that more than anything.

"Dah?" Carla says, coming in closer. "Is something wrong? Did Lucian do something to you?"

"No," I say, my voice thick with emotion. "Not at all." It would be far easier to just tell her my dilemma and not have her guessing at what's wrong, but I can't bring myself to do it. I don't want to risk telling her and being crushed that she doesn't understand.

Carla places both her hands on my shoulders and gazes into my eyes. "What is it then, huh? You can tell me."

No I can't.

The lump is growing bigger. And I don't know why. Everything is happening so fast, and I don't know what to do. Just days ago, I was happy to have finally found someone who could get me off, but now he knows my secret and I think I'm falling for him. Fuck.

Tears well up into my eyes, and I feel like any moment I'm gonna start choking on them.

Seeing the anguish on my face, Carla pulls me into a tight

embrace. "C'mere, girl." She begins patting on my back, not knowing she's making things worse. "Whatever's the matter, it's going to be okay. I'm here for you."

My throat constricted with emotion, I'm unable to say a word, and can only manage to think my response.

Oh Carla, if only you knew.

CHAPTER 21

LUCIAN

The minute I get into the door, I make a beeline for the playroom. I can't wait to see her. I'm ready for training to really begin. I drop the keys on the foyer table, making a loud clinking sound, and start undressing, leaving the jacket on the floor as I make my way to the stairs. I loosen my tie and pull it off as I push open the door, revealing my treasure.

She's still, and in the exact position she should be in. The sight of her gorgeous curves and bared pussy makes my dick that much harder. She stirs slightly when she hears me walk in. I close the door gently, but I'm not nearly as quiet as I have been. She rights herself instantly and goes motionless.

I know exactly what to do with my treasure. I strip down to my slacks as I make my way to the dresser. It's filled with a variety of gear and toys. I have to open three drawers before I get to the one I need. I look over my shoulder and Dahlia is perfectly still, exactly how she should be. There are a few vibrators in this drawer, in all sorts of sizes. A large wand with a round head making it resemble a microphone in its build, bullet vibrators, butt plug vibrators, an egg with a remote. There's something for every mood and whim. A rough hum comes up my throat as I take each one in.

"Good girl, treasure," I say as I place my hands on the edge of the drawer. "How was your day?"

She answers as I keep my back to her while I debate on which one I should choose. "It went well, sir." Her voice is so soft I can barely hear her. "And yours?"

"Speak up."

"And yours?" she repeats herself. I settle on the wand.

"Draining and unfulfilling up until now," I say as I shut the drawer with the wand in my right hand.

"On your back," I give the command as I shove my pants down and kick them off beside the bed. Dahlia's quick to turn on her back. Her breathing is coming in a little quicker now. Her eyes stare at the ceiling, and her arms lay at her side.

"Look at me," I tell her. "I want to see you when I talk to you."

"Yes, sir." A trail of goosebumps runs down her front as she answers me, pebbling her pale rose nipples. It takes a lot of restraint not to suck them into my mouth. But I refrain.

She needs this first.

"We're going to work on what excites you, Dahlia. I'm going to train you and your body, condition you really. I'm going to make you desire me in any way you can have me."

I crawl closer to her and tap on her inner thigh for her to spread her legs, which she obeys immediately.

"I want you to tell me about your fantasies, Dahlia." Her eyes widen, and her body stiffens as I run the tips of my fingers from her clit down to her opening. She's soaking wet. Fuck, the very sight of her makes me want to take her. I'm dying to be inside of her hot pussy, but I have to wait.

Her breathing gets heavy, and she licks her lips. "I can do that."

I run the tip of the wand through her folds. She sucks in a breath of air from the chill of the steel. "You're going to tell me all your fantasies, Dahlia." I turn on the vibrator as it hits her opening. Dahlia's eyes close, and her lips part slightly. She doesn't move though, she knows better than to move. I slowly work it up to her clit, watching her face and her body for her reactions. I want to know exactly where that sweet spot is. Her thighs twitch, and her back arches slightly as I reach the underside of her throbbing clit. *Bingo.*

"But none of the ones you're thinking." I continue my path over and around her clit and then back down. I can see how much she's resisting the need to writhe with pleasure. If I have to, I'll restrain her, but I don't think I'll need to.

"So tell me your fantasies," I say easily, getting comfortable in my position and knowing this may take a while.

"Any?" she asks me.

I shrug and say, "You can. You'll see what they reward you."

She takes in a sharp inhale as I round the sensitive spot and then she starts, "I dream about being alone at night." Her voice is soft and husky. A blush brings color to her chest and face.

"There's a man behind me. I can hear him, but I'm too afraid to turn around so I walk faster, but he catches me." Her breathing comes in quicker, and her body tenses as the vibrator comes closer to where it needs to please.

"He pins me to the brick wall of an alley," her voice goes tight with need, and her thighs tremble as I hold the wand in place.

"Who is this man?" I ask her, my dick hard with need.

"No one, a stranger, I don't know," she answers quickly. She whimpers when I pull the wand away and leave her on edge. The hum fills the room as her eyes snap open and she stares at me with hurt in her eyes.

"Let's try a different one," I tell her. Her mouth falls open, and she swallows thickly as she realizes what I'm doing. She closes her eyes and nods.

Her throat is hoarse as she slowly says, "I... I dream about being on a date." Her forehead is pinched, and I know she's lying. I pull the vibrator away and she doesn't even look at me.

"Don't lie to me, treasure. Next time I'll punish you."

"I'm sorry," she says weakly.

"Maybe I should tell you a story?" I offer, "and you can finish it?"

"Yes please, sir."

"I dream about taking a beautiful girl and locking her in my office at work." Dahlia's eyes snap open, and she looks back at me with a questioning gaze. "She stays under the desk as I sit at my chair."

"Do you think this could be your fantasy?" I ask her.

She nods her head, shifting slightly on the bed. I quicken the pace of the vibrator as she starts her story.

"I wait for you on my knees." She bites down on her lip and then looks back at me. "You take your cock out as you sit down and stroke it. A bead of precum starts to drip," her voice goes a little higher as I put the vibrator to the underside of her clit and hold it there. She struggles to stay still as she continues her story. "I lick it. You moan," her head thrashes to the side. "So sexy when you moan like that." I ease off the pressure and massage circles around her clit. "You love it when I take you in deep. Your hands fist in my hair." Her breathing picks up as I put the vibrator onto her most sensitive spot. Her face scrunches, and her mouth opens wide.

"Keep going, or I'll stop."

Her fingers dig into the mattress as she continues. "You shove your cock down my throat. You push me up and down your dick. I can feel you all the way at the back of my throat!" Her upper body lifts off the bed as she screams out, close to her release.

My dick twitches with the need to give her what she needs, but I can't. Not yet.

"And then I pull out of your mouth." I continue with the story, letting her concentrate on controlling her body. Her breathing comes in harsh pants. "I pull you up, grabbing the hair at the base of your skull."

Her mouth makes a perfect "O" and her body tenses, her neck arches. "And I kiss you. I take your lips with my own," her body trembles and I capture her screams of pleasure as her orgasm crashes through her body. My tongue tangles with hers and I eagerly climb between her legs, shoving my dick into her hot cunt.

Her back bows, and she breaks our heated kiss to scream out into the hot air between us. I buck my hips, slamming ruthlessly into her and riding through her orgasm.

I stare into her eyes, knowing I want that with her. That fantasy. I need it in my life.

I pick up my pace, already feeling my orgasm approaching and watch as the realization of what's just happened crosses her eyes.

I almost say words I don't mean. I'm just caught in the moment. But as she cups the back of my head and crushes her lips against mine, I lose control of everything. I kiss her back with a passion I thought I once knew and I bury myself to the hilt, spilling my cum deep inside of her tight walls.

As the waves of pleasure wrack through me, I ignore the thoughts creeping in. I see her beautiful eyes shining with devotion, and I close my own, wanting to deny what's clearly between us. Our ragged breath mingles as I stare at the nightstand and try to pull myself together.

I purchased her as a distraction. That's all this is. Even as I brace my body on top of hers and catch my breath while she softly kisses my neck, I ignore the feelings creeping into the crevices of my mind.

CHAPTER 22

DAHLIA

"I came for the first time ever without having to think about being forced," I confess to Carla while chewing on a salty french fry, and gazing out into the beautiful skyline through the floor-to-ceiling windows. We're sitting in Explicit Designs' famed cafeteria, enjoying lunch together. Ravenous for once, I'm enjoying a big fat cheeseburger, fries and a vanilla shake, while Carla is having the same thing, except her shake is milk chocolate.

I've finally told Carla about Lucian's habits in bed, though I don't think I've had much choice in the matter.

For the past few days, Carla has hounded me about the details of my relationship with Lucian and I've finally given in to her incessant prying. Mainly because I so badly want to share my dilemma with someone who understands where I'm coming from. I've kept the details to the bare minimum, keeping it casual and not divulging how my world has been completely shaken up. I still feel like I can lean on her though. Like I can trust her and share this little piece of myself with her. Even if she doesn't realize just how much it means to me.

Taking a sip of her shake, Carla chuckles, her eyes alight with mischief. She looks absolutely lovely today sporting a ruby red dress, the hem coming just above her knees and showing off her nice calves, her hair pulled back into a ponytail with a curl on the end, and her nails painted the same color as her dress. Red pumps adorn her feet, and I think she'd give even the most seasoned fashion model a run for her money with how much she's working that outfit. She sure is a vision in red, let me tell you. "So what's so bad about that?"

I shake my head, biting into another fry and doing a little shrug. "I don't know. Don't you think it's weird that I couldn't get off without fantasizing about that before?"

Carla waves a fry at my face as she swallows down a huge gulp of her shake. "Hell no. That's why we're Subs. We like it kinky... and rough. I can see how someone can find it hard to get off without that fantasy." She makes a face. "It's not something that's a problem for me, but I definitely can relate."

The way she's acting makes me want to tell her about the rape, but I fight down the urge.

I've gone this long without telling her, I think to myself, *there's no reason to tell her now. Besides, she just accepts that's it's a fantasy, and that's all she needs to know.*

Carla lets out a little evil chuckle, pulling me out of my thoughts. "Although... Lucian must be a real grandmaster in the bedroom to make you cum without that fantasy."

Lucian.

The very thought of him fills me with hope. And despair.

For the first time ever, I'd cum without the fantasy of being raped. I'm still in shock. It's amazing when I think about it. No one had ever been able to do it. Not even when I've touched myself.

And yet, I still don't know what's going to happen between us. I still don't know if I'll be able to get there continuously without that fantasy. I'm nervous and apprehensive and hopeful, all at once. I'm just a mess.

Carla is smiling at me, mistaking my quietness for something else. "Look at you!" She lets out a little chirp. "I think you're in love."

My mind snaps back to the present, and I focus on Carla's face, wanting to deny it. But I can't; she's right. I'm falling in love with Lucian. But I'm doubting our relationship will ever be anything more than what it is--a contract for sex. And it hurts. "No I'm not," I lie.

Carla laughs at me. "Don't lie to me, Dah. I totally see it in you. The way you look when you talk about him, how you've been acting this past month. Your feelings definitely go beyond the boundaries of a Sub and her Dom. I should know, since the same thing happened to me." She waves her hand at my face as if she's fanning me 'cause I'm burning up. "Face it, Dah, you're done for."

"And you're totally dumb," I growl, causing her to laugh. "Seriously though, I don't know what's going on with us. You know when my contract is up, he can just find a new Sub, right?" A heavy weight presses down on my chest. That's exactly what I keep thinking is going to happen. That he's going to get tired of trying to heal me. Get tired of me being *broken.*

Carla frowns, put off by my pessimistic attitude. She finishes her chocolate milkshake and tosses the cup in the trash. It's ten past one. Our lunch break is over. "Don't say that, Dah. You have to have hope that things will turn out right."

That's the thing, I tell myself, as I finish off my burger and then get up to toss the rest of my meal in the trash, *I don't want to give myself a sense of false hope.*

I spend the rest of the day going over emails and fashion designs in my office, ignoring everything and just focusing on work. I'm just about to close up and head down to the first floor to await my drive over to Lucian's when I receive an unexpected call.

"Hello?" I answered in a guarded voice.

"Dah!" my mother's raspy voice greets me with more pep than I remember. With how scratchy her voice is, I can tell she's been hitting the cigs pretty hard lately, probably up to several packs a day. "Hey honey, how have you been?"

This is the first time in recent memory that I've been ecstatic that my mother's called me. I haven't heard from her in so long, her voice is like music to my ears. It should piss me off that I'm just now hearing from her, but I'm so happy to have someone to talk to. Maybe I can even get the courage to talk to her. She doesn't know about my issues, but I could tell her about Lucian, even if it's not real. I could tell her about the paper and that I'm in a relationship. I want to. I'm dying to talk about it. I don't know why, but I just need to talk to her. "Hey Mom!" I greet her cheerfully, "I've been alright, how have you been?"

"Good, good. I'm glad you're doing okay, honey. I've been worried about you."

I smile. Mom seems like she's called me with genuine concern. I open my mouth to start telling her about my situation, when she cuts me off with, "I got your text." Her voice has dropped several octaves, signaling that her mood has shifted. "I can't really help out in the money department right now," she finishes.

If it weren't so sad, I'd laugh. Figures she'd call when I most likely won't need the help. I part my lips to tell her I should be set for a pretty good while, but then close them, realizing it's probably not wise. I shouldn't tell her about the money, which I haven't received yet. Knowing my luck, she'd try to ask me for some, claiming I owed her a cut for birthing me into this world. And that money is just enough to pay off all my debt. Every cent of it. After taxes I'll have a little left over while I'm waiting to start a real job, something that'll actually pay me. "That's alright, Mom. I worked things out with the school and everything will be fine."

"Oh honey, I'm so happy for you," Mom says, zero happiness in her voice. "I'm so glad you were able to fix things, I really hated having to turn you down."

I want to say something nice in return, but I can't find the words. She really doesn't give me much to work with.

The call goes silent except for the atmospheric static.

"I'm going to see Todd for Christmas," Mom announces when the silence stretches past fifteen seconds.

I perk up at the news. Even though I'm upset with her, I would love to see her. So much has gone on in my life since we last talked, it would be nice to enjoy each other's company. And I still haven't met Todd. I'd like to though. It seems like this must be serious between them.

"Do you want me to come, too?" I ask. In the back of my mind, I'm thinking about Lucian. Our thirty days will be over soon. My heart hurts thinking we could be over, too. Even if we aren't, I don't know if he'd want me around. After all, I'm his Sub. I have to keep reminding myself that.

And he has his own family, I tell myself, remembering the sister he's mentioned to me that he cares so much about, even though he hates his parents. It's something else we have in common. He feels like his parents have done him wrong and I feel likewise, and we both have such screwed-up pasts, though I'd argue mine is a bit more screwed-up than his. Well maybe not more, but different. I almost huff at a humorless chuckle at the thought. Still, Lucian's past gives him special insight on my problem, helps him understand me. He knows what it feels like to be hurt by someone who claims to love you, to be betrayed by the very people you trust.

I hear my mother suck in a breath, bringing me back to the present moment, followed by a long pause. "I don't think Todd wants anyone else coming," she finally admits.

I sit there numbly, letting her words sink in. Why am I not surprised? I should've known better than to ask a question like that. At least she told me ahead of time. For Thanksgiving she told me she was spending it with Todd only a few weeks in advance, too. But that's Thanksgiving, not Christmas. There's a big difference. At least to me there is.

"Oh, that's okay," I say evenly. *I'm not going to break down over this. I'm not going to break down over this.* I have to repeat it over and over in my head.

"I'm really sorry, honey." Surprisingly, I detect faint emotion in her voice. I ignore it, along with my own emotions threatening to consume me.

"It's okay, really. I understand." My voice is even, practically robotic.

"I'll talk to you soon, okay? I have a plane to catch."

"Yeah." Before I can get in another word I hear the line go dead.

Click.

I sit there for a moment, staring at my desk, feeling empty inside. If I could've gotten over leaving Lucian for a while, this would've been the perfect time for Mom and I to bond, for her to listen to me and give me advice on my problems. But that was a fool's fantasy. She hasn't been here for me for so long, and she's not about to start now. I need to get over it and let her come to me when she's ready.

For now, I'll just stay at my apartment for Christmas.

Alone.

Gathering my things, I walk out of my office and head down to the first floor, feeling the unhappiest that I've felt in a while.

CHAPTER 23

LUCIAN

She's late. I came in, and somehow I already knew. When I opened the door and saw the empty bed, my breathing slowed, my blood cooled. Anger wasn't there, but fear was.

She's left me. I'm still standing in the doorway, trying to convince myself that I'm wrong. I know I am. I *paid* for her. She can't leave me. My heart thuds once. She doesn't care about the money. She never has. Not once has she mentioned it. But still. She's not leaving me. My own insecurities are creeping in, and I shove them away.

She's mine. I can take care of her. I am taking care of her. I nod my head and turn from the room.

I let it resonate through me. She's coming. She'll be here. I calm my racing heart and slowly close the door with a gentle click. My palm presses against my pocket, but it's empty. I clear my throat and make my way toward the stairs with a hard expression, devoid of all emotion. I left my phone on the foyer table, but I don't need it. As I hit the last step, I hear the keypad rejecting an entry.

My treasure. I imagine she's panicking in this moment. As I walk to the door, my phone goes off. I stare at it, my hand hovering on the doorknob, but it doesn't matter what her excuse is. She's late.

I open the door, my expression stern and her body jolts some. Her breathing is coming in quick as she takes a half step back.

"Lucian, I-"

"Sir," I correct her with a hard voice. My grip on the door tightens as she stares back at me with her mouth slightly opened. The lines are blurred, and that's obvious. But I'm still her Dom, and she's late and she's hesitating.

I open the door wider and she walks in quickly with her head down. "Thank you, sir," she says uneasily.

I should take her upstairs, but I can't wait. I need her now.

My fingers deftly unbuckle my belt as I walk to the living room. I stand by the sofa and wait for her eyes to reach mine as I pull the belt from the loops. "Strip and bend over," I give her the command and lust covers her expression. She's quick to do exactly what I tell her.

Every second that passes my blood gets hotter, my cock

harder. Her heels slip off her feet as she shoves her dress down. She doesn't hesitate to bare herself to me and bend over the arm of the mahogany leather sofa. She has to balance herself on her toes as her upper body lays flat on the cushion. Her hair fans around her and she looks back at me, the perfect picture of obedience.

My dick pushes against my zipper as I fold the belt in my hand. I run it along her spine and trail it slowly down to her ass. Her eyes close, and she lets out a mix of a whimper and a moan.

"Why are you being punished?" I ask her.

"For being late, for addressing you incorrectly, and for disappointing you and forgetting my place, sir." I close my eyes behind her and let my head fall back.

Perfection.

She's so fucking perfect. I pull back my arm and quickly lash the belt across her ass. It hits her with a loud *smack*! and she lets out a small scream as her hands ball into fists in an attempt not to cum.

"Count them, treasure," I say calmly.

"One, sir," she says loudly.

Smack! I aim just below the soft curve of her ass on her upper thighs. I pull back the blow slightly, knowing it'll be more tender.

"Two!" she yells with her face scrunched up, but her pussy clenches and her mouth opens with desire.

Smack!

"Three," she whimpers.

This one is higher, in a fresh spot and she pushes her ass up to meet the blow. I steady my hand on her lower back to remind her. She needs to be still. The belt whips through the air. *Smack!*

"Four, sir." Four is good. Four is more than enough. She writhes slightly and bites down on her lip.

I drop my belt to the floor, the buckle making a loud clank, and gentle my hands over the marks on her ass. The red lines are slightly raised, and Dahlia seethes in a breath as I press my hand against the hot marks. She presses her ass into my touch and struggles to keep her body from squirming with pleasure. I've administered the perfect amount of pain to give her the endorphin rush she needs.

I eye them carefully, making sure they won't bruise and there are no cuts. Just four parallel red lines.

I lean forward, my hard dick nestled in her pussy, the fabric of my pants separating our hot skin. I graze my teeth along her naked shoulder and nip her earlobe. My hand travels along her waist, her stomach, up to her lush breasts and I squeeze gently and then pinch her nipple as I kiss her lips. Her mouth opens as I pull slightly, my other hand traveling to her soaking wet pussy.

"Thank me for your punishment, treasure," I say with a calmness I don't feel.

"Thank you, sir," she whimpers, struggling to stay still as

I rub her swollen clit and pull on her nipple until it slips from my grip.

The need to punish her pussy and command her body is riding me hard, my thick cock pushing against my zipper as I watch her glistening sex clench around nothing.

I don't know what to do. We both want this, I know that much. But I don't know if it's detrimental to what we're working toward.

She can see my hesitation and her soft eyes flicker with self-doubt. I hate it. I won't allow it. My shortcomings won't cause her pain.

"Is this what you want, treasure?" I ask her in a hard voice, shoving my pants down and stroking my dick. I push her back down and she gasps. Her breathing is coming in ragged pants as she hesitantly looks back at me.

I line my dick up with her hot opening and slam into her. Her tight walls force a rough grunt from my lips as I pound into her mercilessly over and over again.

I push her face down into the cushions and fuck her at an angle that goes deeper than I ever have before. The sofa muffles her screams as I drill into her tight cunt, throwing my head back and groaning at how fucking good she feels.

My toes curl into the carpet as I thrust my hips harder and harder. The sofa shudders each time, and I have to lean forward to keep the heavy furniture from moving too much. Her hips dig into the sofa and her toes come off the floor as

I lose control, slamming recklessly into her, loving how her nails scratch against the leather sofa.

Her body tenses and I know she's close, and that's when I lose focus. Thinking about her. About her pleasure. About her pain. I try to shake the thoughts away, rutting between her legs with a primal need, but I can't shut them out.

Her pussy spasms on my dick and she feels so fucking good, but my mind is racing with the knowledge of why she's just gotten off. Her past and her struggles corrupt every bit of pleasure in my being as she screams out my name.

I can't. I can't get off on this.

I pull away from her, still hard and slipping out, letting her fall limp and sated on the couch, her orgasm still running through her body and making her thighs tremble. She pulls her knees into her chest and tries to calm her breathing as I walk away.

I breathe in deep, running my hand over my face and trying to think. My head is fucked up, and I feel lost. I question taking her like that.

I pace the floor, not knowing how to handle what I've just done. I don't know what's best for her.

The moment she realizes I'm still hard and that I'm not able to cum this way, not knowing why she needs this, her face crumples and she covers her mouth as she's wracked with sobs.

"Treasure," I whisper her name, my heart sinking into my hollow chest. She shakes her head and tries to push me away.

"You don't want me," she says.

I grip her chin firmly and wait for her to look me in the eyes. "I want you. Don't you ever think or say anything differently."

She swallows the lump in her throat. "You couldn't cum," she says just above a murmur.

I don't know how to answer her. "You don't want me like that anymore."

"I fucking love you like that. I love fucking you raw and hard and forcing your pleasure." Her bright eyes finally meet mine again. "Don't think that I don't. I want you every way I can have you. I just... couldn't, knowing."

Her eyes fall, and I hate that I did this to her. I wish I was a stronger man. I wish I had all the answers.

I hook her chin with my finger and bring her lips to mine for a sweet, chaste kiss. But she doesn't return it. Her lips are hard, and her heart's not in it.

"I want you, treasure. I still want you." She needs to believe me. I had a single moment of weakness and doubt. I shouldn't have. But I did.

I brush her tears away with the rough pad of my thumb, hating that I hurt her this way. I can see the regret in her eyes as she takes in a staggering breath and pushes the hair away from her hot face. Her cheeks are red and her eyes are glassed over, and she won't look at me.

I fucking hate it.

I grab her chin in my hand and I force her to kiss me. I crush my lips to hers, my tongue diving into her mouth and massaging against hers. Her small hands grab my shoulders and she kisses me back with just as much force and just as much passion.

I lie on the sofa, pulling her on top of me and gently sliding inside of her hot pussy, still slick with her arousal and cum. I grip her hips tightly and thrust my hips to fuck her with a slow pace. Each thrust is hard and deep, forcing small gasps from her. She places her hands on my chest as I slowly lie flat and continue to fuck her, while she meets me thrust for thrust.

Her tight walls stroke my dick causing a numbing pleasure to grow in the tips of my fingers and toes. I hold my breath as I pick up my pace and pull her down closer to me. Kissing her quickly with a bruising force as I fuck her harder and faster. All the while holding her close to me, where she belongs.

As I close my eyes, letting the pleasure wrack through me, I roughly rub her clit over and over, trying to force her over the edge with me. Hot thick streams of cum fill her and leak between us. Her body is tense and on edge, but when I open my eyes, I can see why she hadn't cum.

She's crying. Her face is buried in the crook of my neck.

My heart shatters as I pull her away enough to see her face and kiss her sweetly.

"Treasure?" I can barely breathe, "Did I hurt you?" My heart thumps slowly as I wait for her to answer. She shakes her head, but she won't look at me. Her inhale is long and shaky.

"I couldn't. I started to think-" a sob is ripped from her throat and she falls into my chest. "I'm sorry, Lucian."

"Shh," I kiss her hair and hold her close.

"I don't want to have to think like that anymore." Her tears fall into my shoulder as I rub her back.

"It's alright, treasure. It's going to be alright."

I hold her as she calms herself, rocking her back and forth and kissing her over and over. My heart clenches with each small sob, but I'm here for her.

I kiss her forehead, breathless and consumed with conflicting emotions. The overriding thought being whether or not I deserve her, whether I'm even worthy of being her Dom. But I want to be. I want to heal her. I *will* heal her. I'll find a way. I lift her small body in my arms, cradling her to my chest. She lays her cheek on my shoulder, neither of us saying anything as I carry her to bed.

CHAPTER 24

DAHLIA

Placing a hand over my eyes, I wince as I lower myself down on the pure white sofa, a throbbing pain pulsing my ass. It hurts like hell. But I still love it. It always reminds me of Lucian, of his dominance. It gives me something to cling to, allows me to momentarily ignore my confused emotions. Yet that lost feeling returns as I sink into the couch.

Which is why I've come to see my therapist. Doctor Sandra Andrews.

She's seated cross-legged across from me, in an oversized tufted leather chair, dressed in a white blouse and blue silk slacks, the outfit complementing the room's pale blue carpet and cream-colored walls, a notepad and pen in her hand. For a therapist, she seems young, but that's one of the reasons I like her so much. She possesses a wisdom that's beyond her years, and through the year she's given me sound advice that I've found to always be on point.

Sandra's gazing at me with concern. Her gentle eyes regard me from behind eyeglasses with thin metal frames. "It's been quite some time since you've checked in, Dahlia," Sandra remarks softly, her smooth voice soothing my ears and calming my anxiety.

"I know," I reply in a soft sigh, my voice sounding small. I clear my throat, feeling slightly nervous, pulling my knees into my chest, wincing slightly as pain pulses my ass. My bare feet sit on the sofa, brushing against the chenille fabric. No shoes is a rule Dr. Andrews has. I guess it keeps the area cleaner, but even more than that, it's supposed to make you more relaxed. I pick at the bit of nail polish on my toenails as a sigh leaves me.

"Are you alright?" she asks, seeing my distress.

I huff a small laugh, resting my chin on my knees and looking up at her. "My Dom punished me with a belt last night." I'm shocked at how easy the words come out. As if it's normal. As if *I'm* normal.

Shifting in her seat, Sandra takes off her glasses. Her brows are pinched as she taps them against her lip. "And how did that make you feel?"

I almost chuckle at how much like a stereotypical therapist she sounds. But I don't have any humor in me. I push my hair out of my face and consider her question. It made me feel alive. And wanted. But that ended far too quickly. Too good to last.

It takes Sandra a moment to realize what caused my reaction, the faint huff of a laugh at her question, and when she does, she sets her glasses down on the end table and shakes her head. "I'm sorry, Dahlia, you've simply caught me a little off guard. Would you mind expanding for me please? I'm not sure what you mean by 'your Dom.'"

It's time to just let it all out. *Let it flow.*

I suck in a deep breath, feeling that oppressive weight on my chest. Slowly, I exhale and begin to tell her everything about Lucian, except I leave out the part about the auction. I know there's doctor-patient confidentiality, but I don't feel comfortable telling her. I don't want to. Sandra listens to me intently while I weave my tale, almost frozen like a statue, her soft eyes compassionate.

"Okay," I say, letting out a soft sigh. I debate on how much information to give her. Our names are in the paper, but I still feel uncomfortable saying his last name. "As you know, I've never been able to get off without fantasizing about being... raped." I swallow thickly as a surge of shame, guilt and worthlessness threatens to overwhelm me, but I squeeze myself tight, warding it off. "But I finally met someone who I felt could help me. Lucian."

"And this man is your Dom?" she asks.

I nod my head, and continue as she jots down notes. "All

I had to do was be his Sub and let him take control, and the rest would come naturally." I look over at Sandra, wondering if she knows enough about BDSM to be familiar with what I'm talking about.

Sandra's very still, but she doesn't look confused, her eyes assessing me inquisitively. "By 'his Sub,' you mean his Submissive?"

So she does know a little something.

I nod my head.

"I see," she says softly, doing a little gesture and then scribbling something on her notepad, "Go on."

I gulp down the lump forming with my throat. "When I became his Sub," I shake my head, my chest feeling increasingly tight, "I finally felt like I was in control, knowing I could stop my fantasy any time I wanted. I could safe word him and it would all stop. I had that power." I sniff, tears burning my eyes. "But at the same time, Lucian had no idea how messed up I was, and he was unknowingly giving me what I thought I needed. Until..." The tears threaten to spill down my face and Sandra reaches for a Kleenex on the decorative stand beside her chair, but I gesture for her to stop. I'm trying to be strong.

"Until?"

"Until he forced my secret out of me," I sigh, my voice a whisper thick with emotion. "I'd been trying to hide it from him from the start, but he knew something wasn't right with me." *Even he could tell I was broken.*

"And what happened next?" Sandra asks.

"He said he could help me." I breathe the words, closing my eyes and remembering. "I was really shocked." I look back at Sandra, and she's nodding. "Up until that point, no one's really understood. My exes sure as hell didn't."

"So, that must've been really encouraging for you then," Sandra remarks. "Knowing that you found someone that not only understood you, but was willing to help you."

God. This lump is growing so big I'm going to choke on it. "Yes," I say and nod my head. "But I didn't really believe it, like, I didn't believe that it would end up working... but then Lucian made me cum for the first time ever without the need of that fantasy." I swallow thickly, feeling like I can't breathe, hoping like hell I can hold it together.

Sandra places the notepad on her lap, her expression brightening, not realizing how I'm about to fall apart. "Why, that's wonderful news, Dahlia." She shakes her head. "That must have been really gratifying, and reassuring. Did that finally give you hope for yourself?'

I close my eyes, feeling a sharp pain pierce my chest, and nod. "It did... for a very short time. And even then, I doubted it. I thought it was a fluke. But then..." I suck in a breath that feels like it's filled with little daggers.

Sandra peers at me intently. "But then?"

I exhale sharply. "Lucian wasn't able to climax when he

was being rough with me, which is how I want him to be with me and it totally," I gulp, "killed what little confidence I had in our relationship. In that moment, I felt like he was disgusted by me."

Sandra's face morphs into a frown. "I'm so sorry, Dahlia." She puts her glasses back on and scribbles in her notepad as she asks, "Did he say why he wasn't able?"

I shake my head no as I answer, "We had sex again, right after that... when he could see I was upset."

"And how did that go?" she asks.

I lean my head back against the sofa and stare at the ceiling. He made love to me, he came and I didn't. Because I'm fucked up and broken. "Not good. He came, but he wasn't rough and so I didn't." My head falls forward and I wait for the doctor's judgment. I just want a solution. I want to be normal.

I'm trying my best not to cry, because I know if I do, this session is over. I won't be able to recover.

"I'm broken," I say just beneath my breath. I could feel something so strong between us, something I've never felt before. But I couldn't give it back to him. I couldn't make love to him. It's so fucked up. It just hurts.

Sandra shakes her head. "No you're not. The progress you made shows that you can recover from this. You *will* recover from this." She gestures at me, her words firm and commanding. "You are a beautiful, talented young woman who's had horrible things happen to her... but that doesn't mean you can't recover, that you can't go on to live a fulfilling normal life." Slightly leaning forward, Sandra's words gain passion as she speaks, so much so that I momentarily forget my pain and focus on her face. After letting her words sink in, she relaxes back into her seat and picks up her notepad. "Now tell me, what's good about your relationship outside of the Submissive and Dom roles?"

Oh," I say, crossing my arms around my torso and clutching myself. I feel so chilly even though it must be seventy-five degrees in this office. "It's... it's really good at times, although it's new and I feel like it's going so fast. He's quiet a lot and it takes some time for him to open up." Sandra nods her head, jotting down notes as I talk.

"He treats me... like... like I mean a lot to him." I finally look her in the eyes. "I know he wants to make me happy."

"And does he?" she asks me.

"Yeah," I say and nod my head. He makes me so happy. "It's so much more than..." my voice trails off. The pain is back again.

"Is it not a relationship beyond the Dominant and Submissive roles?" Sandra presses gently.

"I don't know what to think of it all. I'm confused about where we stand in our relationship. This was supposed to be an..." I fumble for words, not wanting to tell her about the auction. "A temporary arrangement, not something that would turn into anything longlasting. And after that last session..." I shake my head as a surge of emotion chokes my speech. "I don't think we'll ever be able to get past my issues, so all the other aspects don't even matter."

"I disagree with you saying those things don't matter," Sandra says tenderly. "They do matter. If Lucian treats you as good as you say outside the bedroom, and the only problem you're having is the hang-up on your past, I think there's hope here and something you can definitely work with. The question is--is Lucian the man that can do it... and is he willing to commit and stick by you to see you through these issues?"

Numb, I sit there, hugging myself, fighting back those ugly tears. Sandra's right of course, but I don't know what to say. I feel like I'm falling for Lucian, but in doing so, have set myself up for a broken heart. Lucian is a very rich man, with very many options. He could easily one day decide I'm not worth the effort and find himself a new Submissive. Or I may only ever be a Submissive to him. I want more. But I want it from him.

"I don't know." I whisper the answer.

"What I would suggest," Sandra says softly, pulling me out of my thoughts, "is having an honest talk with Lucian about what your wants and needs are. If you want him to commit to you, tell him that. And expect him to give you an answer on it. Otherwise, despite the progress you've made, this relationship could be harmful and cost you a lot of emotional and mental distress." She sets the notebook down and says,

"This is just my opinion, but it seems as though there's more than a Dom/sub relationship and that's what's driving these changes for you. Make sure that's the case, and work together to continue your progress."

I don't know what to say. I feel so tense and on edge. I'd be asking him for more. I don't think it's an option. He's going to leave me or just fuck me until the contract is over. I cover my heated face with my hands and try to just focus on me. I want this. I'm scared to death to ask him for this, but I want to. I have to. But he's already given me so much. He's showed me it's possible. I'm so conflicted.

"Go talk to him, Dahlia." Sandra's words make my eyes snap to hers. "Let him know what you need. I hope he can continue to help you and that you're able to work on this foundation you've built."

I hope so, too, I think to myself feeling growing resolve as I leave her office and knowing that there's only one thing left to do.

CHAPTER 25

LUCIAN

I'm no good for her. I've already come to terms with it. I don't know how to help her. I know some of my own desires and needs could harm her. Emotionally, psychologically. I want to be strong enough for her. I want to have the experience to know how to heal her.

But I don't have all the answers. My heart clenches, knowing I should let her go. Cut ties from the contract and make sure she gets the help she needs from someone else. I keep hurting her. I don't mean to, but I know that I am.

I clench my jaw and pull out my cell phone, waiting on my sister to get here. I'm in the same spot that I was before. The same cafe we always come to. Today it's darker. The grey clouds block the sun and rain threatens to start falling at any second, but I don't care. I'm staying outside. At least for now.

A glance at my phone shows a text from Isaac.

It's done.

My body stiffens slightly, and adrenaline spikes through my blood.

Her uncle is dead.

That bastard took my treasure's innocence. Even worse, she wasn't the first and she wasn't the last.

The law gave him five years in prison, that's all. And he never even went to trial for what he did to my treasure. That's not justice. And the last girl, the second one he was prosecuted over after hurting Dahlia, was his neighbor; there wasn't enough evidence for the judge to proceed, but I know the truth. I saw what they had on him. I read the testimonies. He needed to die.

I should feel guilty, and maybe I should even be disgusted with myself. But I don't feel a damn thing other than satisfied. He hurt my treasure in a way I know I can never fully understand.

"Your coffee, sir." The waitress flashes me a sweet smile, her cheeks a bright red from either the chill or more blush than necessary. "Can I get you anything else?" she asks, leaning in slightly. Too close for my comfort.

"No, thank you." I'm short with my words, and the look on her face falls. Again, I should care. But I don't.

"Lucian!" My sister appears from behind the waitress, sparing me whatever looks the young woman was giving me.

She wraps her arms around my shoulders, not even giving

me a moment to stand.

I always look forward to seeing Anna. But as I look down to click my phone off and ignore the text message, I feel... broken. Everything is off-center and an emptiness fills my chest.

She squeezes me one more time and looks for the waitress, but she's gone.

I huff a humorless laugh as Anna pouts and almost shrugs off her coat, but decides against it, falling into her seat and looking past me, into the cafe.

When her eyes reach me once again, that bright smile lights up her face. "You have a girlfriend," she says, and her voice etched with awe.

I pick up my coffee and blow on it, not knowing how to handle this. I don't give a fuck what anyone thinks really. Zander and Isaac know the truth. My sister's the only other person in my life who matters. But I'm sure as fuck not going to tell her the truth.

She leans across the small table and playfully smacks my arm as I set the cup down.

"Come on," she urges me, "spill it!"

Her excitement brings a small smile to my face, although it doesn't reflect what I'm feeling at the moment. "She's a sweet girl, but I'm not sure how serious it is." *Lies.* I tell my sister lies. I've never been more serious about anything in my life. But I know I'm not good for her. I don't know if I can keep her.

"She's so pretty!" Anna's eyes go wide and she lets out a soft sigh. "I can see it in your face," she says, and her voice is teasing.

I grunt out a laugh. "Leave it be, Anna."

"You'll bring her to the Christmas party?" she asks me. The hopeful look on her face is too much. Christmas is less than three weeks away. I already turned her down for Thanksgiving. I'd only just gotten my hands on my treasure, and with neither of us committed to spending the holiday with family, I made sure she spent it on her knees. It was the most successful holiday I've had in years.

"I have no idea if we'll still be seeing each other by then." As I say the words, I realize how much pain they cause me. The very thought that my treasure may be gone in less than a month physically hurts. Doubt and uncertainty are two emotions I don't handle well.

"Tell me, how are your classes going?" I ask quickly to change the subject.

"Are you high?" she asks incredulously. "It's Christmas break." I take a sip of the bitter black coffee, wishing this meeting were over. I have three conferences left today and only then can I go home and take care of her.

"So, Mom called me." Anna's words bring me back to the present.

I can feel my facial expression harden as I wait for more.

"She said she's sorry."

It takes a lot for me not to roll my eyes at my sister's naiveté. She's a sweet girl and I love her, but she's a fool.

"What else did she say?" I ask, although I can't keep my voice even.

She looks hurt by my harsh tone and I instantly regret it.

She softens her voice and says, "She's really sorry." Her eyes plead with me, but I can't. I won't.

"'I'm sorry, Anna," I shake my head and look away, "I can't-"

She quickly reaches across the table, taking my hand in both of hers as she continues, "I'm not asking you to do anything. I promise you." My heart clenches looking at the tears in my sister's eyes.

"I know what they did, and it was wrong. I just wanted you to know..." her voice cracks, and she sucks in a breath. "But I know you don't trust them," she says as her face falls.

I stand up and hug my sister close, rubbing her arm as she holds me back.

I hate that she's so emotional and pulled in different directions. "It's alright, Anna." She's put herself in the middle of this feud. She's suffered from both sides. I went a long time without seeing her. I regret it, but at the time I didn't want to be reminded of what I'd lost. I wish I could take it back. I wish I could protect her from what happened.

"I love you, Lucian." She looks up at me, brushing away the one stray tear rolling down my cheek. "I hope you know that."

I nod my head once, holding her gaze.

"I have to go, Anna."

She gives me a quick squeeze and regains her composure.

I hate that I have to leave her like this. But I have no solutions for her.

She sniffles and looks past me for the waitress as I put two twenties on the table and lean in to kiss her forehead.

"Take care, Anna," I tell her as I turn away from her.

"You too," she whispers.

This fucking meeting is never going to end. And it's only the first of the three I need to take care of before the day is over. I'd run my hand over my face, but it's a video conference. So instead I stare straight ahead, listening to the pros and cons of moving the manufacturing of casings for the new prototype to South Korea while leaving the remainder in the US.

I need the numbers and I need the statistics, but what I don't need is the two heads of the two opposing divisions to get into a fucking argument and take up my time.

I finally speak up, putting an end to this nonsense. "Mr. Crenshaw, I fail to see the point of this debate."

"It's about timing, Mr. Stone. This is going to destroy my timeline."

"The bottom line is what matters," Mr. Jenkins answers in a stern voice.

There's a knock at the door, interrupting the conference. I ignore it.

Knock knock, it comes harder this time.

Crenshaw and Jenkins continue to debate on whether or not their shipping methods are reliable and I look up to the door as I say, "Come in." Linda knows my schedule and she should know better than to interrupt me, especially when the head of my development department is telling me my timeline may be fucked because of this change.

I glance at the door when it opens, and I have to do a double take.

"Dahlia?" I look up past the monitor and ignore the conference. Their voices pour from the speakers, but it's white noise. Dahlia's in my doorway, with Linda right behind her.

"Mr. Stone," Linda says with an uneasiness as she looks between the two of us. "I wasn't-" she starts to explain herself, but I wave her away.

"Leave us."

Dahlia looks unsteady. She seems lost with what to do with herself. I wait for her to tell me what's going on. Or to come over to me, but she just stands in the middle of my office, twisting her hands around the strap of her purse. With doubt in her eyes and uncertainty clear on her face.

My forehead pinches with confusion. What the hell is she doing here? *It looks like she's been crying.* The realization snaps something inside of me.

I stand abruptly from my desk, and it's only then that I hear the voices coming through. It was all white noise before.

"Mr. Stone," several men call out. Fuck. I look back at the monitor gritting my teeth, but the moment I do, Dahlia turns to leave.

"I'm sorry, I shouldn't have-"

"Stay." I give her the command, and she freezes. Her breathing is coming in harsher than before.

I walk past her to the office door, ignoring the questions coming through the speakers, and lock it before moving to the blinds and closing them all. I can feel Dahlia's eyes on me, but I don't turn to face her gaze until we have privacy.

"When Mr. Stone..." a voice rings through the speakers and I quickly walk over to the other side of the desk and lean forward, hitting mute and exiting out of the conference without a word. I don't owe them an explanation, and they still need to have this sorted by tomorrow at the latest. I pay them well, and I expect no less from them.

"Lucian, I-" Dahlia finally says as I walk toward her. I take her small hands in mine and bring her closer to me.

"What's wrong?" I ask her.

"I shouldn't have-" she looks down at the grey carpet and shakes her head, the doubt and regret spreading through her.

I hook my finger under her chin and tilt her up so her soft hazel eyes are forced to look back at me. "What's wrong?"

"I..." She's so hesitant. Last night was hard on us, and I failed her. Again. This is my fault. "I feel like," she chokes on her words, looking past me and out of the window. "I need more."

"I'm sorry about last night," I apologize to her. Her eyes widen slightly as I lead her to the sofa on the side of the office. "Please forgive me for not being as strong as I should be. I've never..." my voice trails off slightly as I debate on how to word this.

"I need to find a balance between giving you what you need, and fulfilling your desires." I pull her into my lap and rub soothing circles along her back. "I also need to curb some of my desires, treasure. And last night that's where I failed you." I cup her chin in my hand and place a soft kiss on her lips.

"I can be a better Dom for you. I will." The look in her eyes is filled with uncertainty. My heart beats frantically at the realization. "Tell me what you're thinking," I command her.

"I want that," she says softly. But there's still hesitation clearly present in her expression.

"What else do you want?" I ask her.

She's quiet and obviously worried, and I don't know why. Maybe she's lost faith in me. I won't let her think that. I won't let her slip through my fingers.

"Get on your knees," I tell her. I'll make her see how good this is. I won't let her question it. I know I failed her, but I can make this right.

Her lips part with a small gasp and she crawls off of me, keeping her eyes on mine until her knees are on the carpet and her hands rest on her thighs.

"Good girl," I say and her expression lifts with my praise.

I slowly unbuckle my belt and pull out my cock. I stroke it once and her eyes dart to it and then back to mine.

I keep stroking my dick, making her wait for it. The heated look in her eyes and the quickening of her breathing only makes me harder. It feels like velvet over a thick steel rod in my hand. I groan as a bit of precum leaks from the tip.

"Lick," I utter, and the second the command comes out, her hot tongue laps at my head and she cleans it off with a deep moan. Her beautiful eyes look up at me while she continues to obey me, and it's all I can take.

She wants it hard and rough, and so do I. I can give her that and keep her from taking this to a dark place that she doesn't want to go.

I will.

I pull her up by her hips and throw her down on the sofa, pulling her skirt up over her waist and ripping her panties down her thighs. I can't get them off fast enough, and the thin lace tears. Her neck arches at the sound, and her glistening pussy clenches.

I spread her thighs wider, and slam into her tight pussy without warning. Her back bows at the intensity, and she screams out.

"You'll be quiet, treasure." Her wide eyes look back at me as she bites down on her lip, and I quickly lean forward, fucking my treasure on the leather sofa with short fast strokes. My fingers dig into her hips with a bruising force as my lips crash against hers.

Soft moans mingle with our hot breath and she struggles now to writhe under me as I pound harder into her. My pants fall down around my ass as I pick up my pace, thrusting into her with a savage force, all the while kissing her with devotion and holding her close.

I can give her both. I can, and I will.

"Lucian," she moans my name as her head falls back. Fuck, the sound of her voice full of pleasure, and the feel of her tight walls, hot and wet with her arousal makes me groan into the crook of her neck. I want to nut between her thighs with the primal desire I feel for her. I want to let loose and take from her. But I don't. I can't. I force myself to stay in control and grip the back of her neck as I whisper against her lips.

"Cum for me, treasure." Her eyes stare into mine as I slide in and out of her slick pussy easily, with a force that makes her gasp slightly. Her body jolts with each hard thrust. Every time she closes her eyes, I kiss her gently, passionately, with everything I have.

I'm on edge and ready to cum. It's hard not to with how good she feels. My toes curl, and I hold it back. Her first. I need this from her. She needs this.

"Cum for me," I command her again, slipping my hand between our bodies and rubbing her swollen clit.

Dahlia's eyes go half-lidded and her lips part as her head falls back. I can see she's close, so close. I lean forward, spearing my fingers through her hair, maintaining my steady pace and bringing her forehead close to mine.

I fist her hair and pump my hips faster, gazing into her eyes. There's a spark there, staring back at me, keeping me focused on her. Soft moans pour from her lips and I'm quick to muffle them with my kisses. Our tongues tangle in a heated need to be as close to one another as we can. Her arms wrap around my shoulders, her hands in my hair as I thrust deeper, jolting her body slightly.

I tighten my grip on her hips as she pulls away, moaning my name. Her neck arches, and her mouth opens as her pussy spasms around my dick. I groan into the crook of her neck, loving the feeling and needing more. I kiss along her neck and up her jaw to her lips.

She greedily kisses me back with a passion I've never felt, her hot breath filling my lungs. Her fingers dig into my back, pulling me closer to her. And I lose my composure. "Treasure," I murmur reverently, kissing every available surface of her soft skin as I thrust into her again and again, until I reach my own climax.

The tingling pleasure rolls through my body, building with a tension in the pit of my stomach and then explodes outward. My eyes close and I pull away from her as a rough moan is torn from my throat, but Dahlia takes my head in her hands and forces me to kiss her. She presses her soft lips to mine, and I give her everything I have.

She takes every bit of me in that moment. It's all for her.

CHAPTER 26

DAHLIA

I walk through the hallway of Lucian's penthouse, my chest heaving with excitement, my heart pounding with anticipation. I'm feeling nauseated, and I don't know what from.

Things are different. Yesterday was different. The rules have changed. At least for me they have. I was too chickenshit to tell him that I want him as a partner, a boyfriend, whatever he wants to call it. I need more than a Dom. But I think he knows that. Maybe I'm just pretending. Playing house so that I don't have to believe that I'm just his pet. Just a Submissive he bought at the auction. It feels like so much more though, at least to me.

I'm too afraid to put a label on us. I'm afraid of what he'll say.

I key in the code and open the door. Just like I've done

every day for almost a month, it feels natural. Setting my purse on a stand in the foyer, I stop for a moment to touch the necklace at my throat. Lucian gave it to me this morning. It's beautiful, made of gold and diamonds and has a bold, but elegant thickness to it. He wants me to be collared at all times. And he's obtained a variety of them for me. I'm spoiled. I'm very well aware that he's spoiling me in the jewelry department.

Reaching up behind my neck, I delicately take off the chain and slip it into my purse, grabbing out my new Sub collar in its place and locking it around my neck. This one is even more beautiful, with spiked diamonds and gorgeous gold accents dotting the sumptuous, cream-colored leather. It's very flashy, and I would never wear it unless I was alone with Lucian.

I continue down the hallway on my way to the playroom, when I see him standing at the foot of the double-sided staircase. My breath catches in my throat at the sight of him. He's never home when I get here. I'm supposed to wait for him. For a moment fear grips my chest, and I think I must be late. But he smiles at me as he walks toward me. No hint of a punishment in sight. He's looking fucking hot as hell this afternoon, which shouldn't be surprising since I saw him earlier this morning and he looked fucking hot as hell then, too.

It's obvious he's been waiting for me, and I've shown up exactly when he wants me to. My pulse begins to pound between my ears, and my legs tremble slightly as his gaze falls on me.

I quickly kneel, falling easily to the floor and submitting to him. I place my hands on my thighs and wait for him obediently. It's the position he first made me get in on our first day. The memory puts a small smile on my face.

"Come here, treasure," he commands in a voice I can't deny.

I drop onto all fours and slowly begin crawling my way over to my Dom. It feels awkward. I've never crawled to him before, but I'm his Sub right now and I think this is what I'm supposed to do. I don't want to mess up. I jolt slightly when he commands me to stop, his voice harsh.

"Don't crawl," he says, a hint of irritation in his voice. "I don't want to play right now. Get up and walk over to me."

Ashamed, I climb to my feet, my cheeks burning. I hesitate, feeling insecure now, my anxiety returning.

"Now, treasure," he demands with even more authority.

My stomach twisting with apprehension, I walk over to stand in front of him. Up close, I can see something's off about him. His whole body seems tense and he looks like... just worn down, like he's had a rough day. At least, I hope that's what it is.

My contract is almost over. Maybe he's about to tell me he doesn't want to renew it. That he's ready to move on.

I'm filled with nausea over these thoughts, and it's hard to keep my composure. Before I can ask him what's wrong, he pulls me into him, kissing me on the lips passionately. Sighing softly, I melt into his arms, letting him hold me, surrendering my entire body to him.

When Lucian pulls back, my chest is heaving as I release breathless pants. That kiss was intense, and it goes a long way in calming me. Lucian obviously isn't calling things off. Yet.

"What was that all about?" I ask breathlessly.

"You asked for more. That was me giving you more." I try to respond, but I'm not sure how. I didn't expect this. This can't really be happening.

I part my lips to say something, anything, but Lucian places his fingers against them, quieting me. "Shhh. This is about me and you right now. Let me give you what you asked for. We're not going to the playroom tonight. Tonight, it's just *us*."

Just us? I stare at him in shock, hardly trusting what he's offering. Lucian appears to be dangling everything I could ever want, right in front of me. I should be jumping for joy, yet I'm still worried that this is all some sort of cruel joke.

"Will that make you happy, treasure?" he asks, looking me straight in the eyes and making me weak in the knees. I can't believe it. I want to clarify what more means to him. But I can't. I'm afraid of the answer, and the deadline approaching us.

"Yes... Lucian," I respond softly.

"You're doing well," Lucian whispers in my ear, his breath hot on my neck as he places his large hands atop mine and gently guides them in kneading the big ball of dough on the cutting board in front of us.

For dinner, Lucian wanted to pass on takeout and bond over making homemade pizza. I was apprehensive about it as I've only made it a few times before, and it's never turned out well. But Lucian assured me it would be fine, that I had all I needed, chiefly him to guide me. Turns out he was right, the dough is almost perfect. And the experience has been one of the most pleasant things I've done in a while.

I could learn to love this, I think dreamily, enjoying the sensation of Lucian's closeness.

A soft sigh escapes my lips as I'm pulled out of my thoughts and feel the heat of his body behind me, his hands guiding mine in a very sensual and deliberate manner, and his big hard dick pressing up against my ass.

"Do you like that, treasure?" Lucian says in my ear, nibbling on my neck, gyrating his cock gently up against my ass cheek, while pressing my hands into the soft dough, molding it into a flat surface.

"Yes," I moan, my pussy clenching repeatedly with need. "Please give it to me, sir."

Lucian kisses me several more times on the neck before saying, "Uh-uh, treasure. Not until we finish this pizza." He huffs out a small chuckle in my ear. "Or at least get it in the oven."

I feel like this is cruel and unusual punishment, pressing his big cock up against me, and then telling me I can't have it until we finish. But I know better than to argue. I just need to get this pizza crust done pronto, throw on the sauce and toppings: pepperoni, sausage, bell peppers, onions, four cheeses, and then throw it in the oven. So I can get all of that big fucking cock.

I continue to let Lucian guide me with molding the dough, and by the time we finish the crust I'm completely covered in flour. But worse than that, my panties are soaked.

"See, treasure?" Lucian asks, stepping out from behind me and filling me with disappointment. Unlike me, Lucian only has flour on his hands and a little bit on his blue apron. He nods at the crust we made and places it on the pizza pan next to the cutting board. "That wasn't so bad, was it?"

I shake my head, blushing, wishing he were still behind me. "No, I enjoyed it. A lot."

Lucian gives me a hooded look filled with desire, and a promise of what is to come and my breath quickens. "As did I."

I blush harder and I'm about to reply when my cell, which is lying on the end of the counter, goes off with rapid dings. Lucian glances at it and then gives me a look.

I shrug, wiping my hands off with the towel and wondering if it's my mom. Maybe she changed her mind about Christmas.

Before I can take two steps, my phone goes off several more times and I pause. It's unusual I get that many texts in such rapid fashion. Maybe I should check to see who it

266 WINTERS & LANDISH

is. Wiping my hands on a dishrag, I walk over and pick up the phone, but I almost drop it a second later when I see the series of texts, a cold chill striking my spine.

"Oh my God," I gasp, my heart pounding wildly in my chest, dropping my phone to the counter.

Lucian tears his eyes away from the stove and settles them on me. "What's wrong?" he asks with concern.

I place a hand over my chest to calm my rapidly beating heart. "Those texts I just got... they were from my mom."

Lucian goes rigid and he clenches his jaw, but I'm too freaked out to really respond to his strange reaction. "And?" he asks.

I take a deep breath, trying to calm my pulse. "She said my uncle was found dead..." my voice trails off as my mind races in disbelief. My blood heats, and my breath is coming in short pants. The person who'd caused me so much grief is now dead. It doesn't even sound real. *He's gone.*

Lucian doesn't immediately respond, but I take his silence as shock.

"I can't believe it." The words fall from my lips as I read the texts over and over.

I glance at Lucian, noticing that his entire demeanor has changed. The playfulness I enjoyed while we made the crust is gone.

His face is emotionless. I've seen the look before. It's his mask. He's hiding what he truly thinks. A wave of a chill runs through my body, turning my blood to ice. I almost ask him if he knew. He doesn't look surprised. He seems to be waiting for something. Or hiding something.

My heart thuds hard in my chest as I tear my eyes away from him. The thoughts in my head are just paranoia; horrible suspicion pressing down on my chest, a suspicion I desperately don't want to believe.

"Lucian?" I say his name as a question although I can't ask what I really want to know. Something deep down in the pit of my stomach is telling me he did this. Maybe he's not the one who pulled the trigger. But Lucian murdered him.

I swallow thickly as his heavy footsteps approach me.

I have to hold on to the counter to keep myself upright, suddenly feeling like I'm going to faint.

"Are you alright, treasure?" Lucian asks, concern returning to his voice as he walks over and wraps his arms around me, holding me close. I feel awful for leaning into him. For even thinking he did this. *The club is full of powerful men. You don't want to be their enemy.* Carla's words echo in my head as he rubs soothing circles on my arm.

Swallowing back a wave of uncertainty, I reply, "I'm fine."

CHAPTER 27

LUCIAN

I haven't taken a day away from the office in a very long time. But there was no way I was going to leave Dahlia today. We only have today and tomorrow left.

I still have work to do, and so does she, but as soon as I'm finished, she's all mine.

My treasure is waiting for me in the living room. The last I saw her she was sprawled out on the rug with several textbooks and sketchpads, preparing for her final semester and an event for work.

My body relaxes as I remember how she asked me to go with her. She's still coming around to being open with me and telling me what her needs are, but she's doing much better now. It was so obvious that she thought I'd say no, but she's my priority.

I open the desk drawer and take out the contract. I need to extend it, and I've been typing up the language for my half of the contract for the last hour. I've been distracted by the incessant phone calls from PR and my lawyer. I couldn't care less at this point. If my ex is going to publish her tell-all, I'll sue her. I'm not giving her another penny. They don't seem to agree with my tactic, but I don't care anymore.

I'm done with her. Tricia is my past, and that's where she'll stay. If she wants to publish lies, then she can make herself a liar and wind up in court.

I sigh heavily and hate that I've given any more energy to her at all. My head is pounding with a relentless headache. My temples throb with pain that just isn't leaving. I take another two Advil from the bottle on my desk and wash it down with my coffee.

It's almost room temperature now, but I only need the caffeine. A smile graces my lip when my fingers run over the engraving on the outside of the steel mug. *Please, sir.*

She thinks she's cute, my treasure. And she is.

My heart swells for a moment, but then my computer pings with yet another email. This one is from the executives that head up development.

I put my mug down on the desk, intent on getting to work and tying up these loose ends. Once I'm done for today, I'm going on vacation. I want time for just the two of us. She'll be busy once school starts, but until then, her time is mine. And

I want it all. Linda's processing applications for another two executive assistants. I need to start delegating more work. It's a slow going process, but I'm working on it.

I focus on the tasks at hand and make the final decisions on several contracts with ease. Knowing that once this is done with, I'll be able to enjoy my treasure makes the time go by quickly.

A timid knock at the office door makes my fingers pause on the keyboard.

"Come in."

Dahlia peeks her head in, only partially opening the door. "Are you busy?"

I have a moment." I really do need to get this shit done. But I can put it on pause for her.

She walks easily to the desk and I turn my chair so she can sit on my lap. I love the feel of her body against mine. Her warmth and gentle touches soothe me.

I lay a hand on her thigh and plant a small kiss on her neck.

"Will you be done soon?" she asks me. Tricia used to ask me that all the time. At first, anyway. She stopped a few months into the marriage, when she gave up.

I close my eyes and pinch the bridge of my nose. The headache is coming on full force now. I hate that the thought of Tricia ever came to my mind because of something my treasure said. They're nothing alike.

"I have another two hours at least," I tell her, knowing that it'll possibly be more, but I'll come back and finish once she's gone to bed. I'll make time for her. I'm committed to that.

"I was going to make dinner," she wraps her arms around my shoulders, "or maybe order something?"

"What do you want?" I ask her. A sweet smile slips into place on her lips.

"That's what I came in to ask you." I hug her waist closer to me, her ass slipping against my cock and stirring desire. I nip her neck and debate on taking her now. Sating her so she can relax while I finish this.

"What's this?" she asks, her forehead pinched.

I glance down at the contract on the desk. "It's not ready yet. It's the new contract."

She picks up the papers and skims through them.

My body tenses as the crease in her forehead becomes deeper and the look of unhappiness is evident in her eyes.

"I don't want to sign this," she says finally. Her voice is full of apprehension and soft with doubt. But she looks back at me, setting the papers down with strength and finality. She shakes her head. "I don't want to sign it."

I didn't expect that. My body chills at how resolute her decision is. "Do you want more money?" I ask her, not knowing what other problems she could have with it. I've put in her needs. I know I'll meet them. These past few days have been nothing but perfection.

Dahlia pushes away from me and climbs off of my lap, her

warmth leaving me wanting her. I grip her hips to keep her from leaving me but she slaps me away, catching me by surprise.

I quickly rise from my desk, the chair falling backward onto the floor. A touch of fear flashes in her eyes as she walks backward.

I raise my hands, although my voice is strong and my eyes are narrowed. "Dahlia," I say and her eyes fly to mine. She looks angry, but more than that, upset.

"What's wrong?" I ask her, although I'm not a fucking idiot. I shouldn't have implied that it was about money. It's a habit of mine. It's hard breaking them, but I know my treasure better than that. It's not about the money for her. I should have known that.

"I don't want your money," her voice cracks slightly as she crosses her arms and looks away. "I'm not-"

"I'm sorry." I walk toward her, slowly moving my hands around her hips. I can tell she wants to push me away, she wants to leave, but she's my Submissive.

She should have known better than to leave me like she did. She knows better than that. But then again, I knew better than to bring up money.

"Look at me," I say and as the words leave my lips, she obeys. A small frown mars her beautiful face. "Whatever you want to change in the contract, just let me know."

She shakes her head, and her face crumples. "I don't want a contract."

My grip on her tightens, and my heart races in my chest.

"I don't know why you want this if we're... if we're more than this." Her voice is shaky, and she's obviously extremely upset. I don't understand why though.

I hate that she's questioning me. I need contracts. Whatever she wants to change, I can alter. I don't mind that.

"I want this, treasure. I need this." I understand it's fucked up. But I do. I need to know that when I make her angry, or when I fail her, she can't leave me. I need to know she'll still be here and I'll be able to make it right.

"This is what I want from you... equality," she stresses the last word and I still don't understand. I don't get what this has to do with the contract or anything for that matter.

"You are my equal. How can you not see that?"

"I'm your Submissive. I can't be both!"

"You are my Submissive, my other half and my equal. They're all one and the same." It pisses me off that she would think less of herself.

She looks lost again. I'll show her what it means to be mine. My everything. She's best when she submits. She's more comfortable in that role. This questioning everything isn't what she needs.

"I'll change whatever you want, and you'll sign the contract." I'm forceful with her. It's what she needs, I know it is.

"Now get on your knees." She just needs a hard fuck. I've been too busy for her. I won't make the same mistake I made with Tricia, not with her. I can't let her get away from me. I won't let my treasure slip through my fingers.

She looks back at me with uncertainty. "Did you kill him?" she asks me.

My heart stops in my chest, my blood running cold. She hasn't asked. She hasn't brought it up since she got the text messages from her mother. I could tell she knew. It has to be obvious.

"Where's this coming from?" I ask her.

"That's not an answer." Her voice is low, and wavers.

"I'm your Dom, you'll do well to remember that right now."

"I thought you said I was your equal?" she asks as she cocks a brow at me, her voice broken and raw. My heart twists in my chest.

"Yes, you are, and yes, I had him killed." The words slip from my lips before I can stop them, my heart beating so hard it slams with pain on each beat.

She gasps and steps back slightly. My breathing comes in ragged as I wait for her response. I never intended on telling her. I didn't want her to have to carry the weight of knowing. But I won't lie to her.

"He deserved to die, Dahlia. Not only for what he did to you, but what he continued to do after." My words are full of conviction, but she doesn't respond.

She looks toward the door, but I don't want her to leave me. She's scared, and I can comfort her. I can make this right.

I breathe out deeply. "I need you to understand that you're safe. I'll always make sure you're safe."

Her breathing comes in quicker, and she looks so lost. She's forever lost and insecure. If only she'd listen to me. "Come here."

"No," she's quick to respond, and it pisses me off.

I narrow my eyes at her. "Treasure," I say and my voice holds a note of admonishment. She's going to be punished for deliberately disobeying me.

"You're not leaving, Dahlia." I won't let her go. I can't. I can't lose her.

"I have to." I close my eyes at her words, hating them. My hands ball into fists at my side.

"You don't have to do a damn thing but do as I say. Come here."

"Don't make me stay. Please, don't make me stay." My body heats with anxiety at the fear in her voice. She's afraid of me. Tears leak from the corners of her eyes. No. I shake my head, denying that this is even a reality. This wasn't meant to hurt her. I only meant to give her justice.

"It's me, Dahlia. I'm still the same man I was."

"You killed him?" There's a mix of disbelief, fear, and something else in her voice.

I nod my head once. "I hired the hit." Regret starts to creep in, but I refuse to allow it. I had to do the right thing. I only wish she'd understand.

"Come here." I soften my voice, waiting for her Submissive side to come through. I take two steps toward her and she backs away.

"Red." My lungs stop working as she whispers the word, shaking her head. She walks to the door, her soft footsteps echoing in the room and I let her go, standing still and just trying to breathe.

She just needs time. The door closes behind her and I try to move, but I can't. She safe worded me. She left me.

She just needs time. I take in a ragged breath.

I knew that her uncle's death would affect her. I want to be there for her. I know what she needs.

But she doesn't trust me yet. She hasn't given herself fully to me.

I sink into my chair, hating that I had to let her leave, but knowing I'll have her back. She can't leave me. I know she loves me. I fucking love her, too. I'll give her whatever she wants. I just need her back.

Chapter 28

Dahlia

I *can't believe he did it.*

I suck in a deep breath of guilt as I drive to Sandra's office in my beat-up, piece of shit Mazda. I should be incredibly upset about what Lucian did. I'm still trembling. It's one thing to have suspicions, it's another thing entirely to have them confirmed. I wish I'd just lived in denial.

He murdered someone on my behalf. But ever since getting over the initial shock, I feel relieved that the person who caused me so much pain is gone from the world. I'm a horrible fucking person for being happy with his death. I'm torn and conflicted. I need help. I'm not okay.

I suck in another deep breath as I turn off the highway,

taking the road that will take me straight to Sandra's office.

I'm free. Tears prick at my eyes. I hadn't realized how much pain I was in just knowing that man was still breathing. I feel... relief. And guilt.

And what about Lucian? I don't know how to feel. *But nothing matters without him.*

The thought causes a large lump to form in my throat and tears to sting my eyes.

When I step into Sandra's office, she's waiting for me in her leather tufted chair, her legs crossed in front of her, her notepad and pen in hand. It's after hours, but when I called she said she'd be here. She'll never know how much that means to me. Her hair is loose in her bun and her cream-colored blouse is a bit wrinkled from being worn all day, but she's here for me.

"Dahlia," she greets me warmly with a gentle smile. She gestures at the couch across from her. "Please, have a seat."

"Thank you," I say softly, feeling nervousness start to set in, and trembling slightly. Barefoot, I walk over and sink onto the couch, pulling my legs up under me, sucking in a deep breath and exhaling slowly.

"Now, would you like to tell me what's bothering you?" Sandra asks me when I'm fully seated, her soft voice soothing the turmoil that's roiling beneath the surface. Her pale blue eyes focus on me behind her glasses.

I open my mouth to speak, but then close it when I realize something critical I missed on the way over. *I can't tell her anything that will incriminate Lucian, so I'm going to have to be very careful talking about my uncle's death.* I sit there for a moment, my mind racing on what I could safely disclose. I run my hand over my face, hating this and hating everything.

"Dahlia?" Sandra prods gently.

"My uncle is dead," I announce, suddenly deciding that I will just go with a variation of the truth. Hopefully Sandra won't read too much into it.

Sandra lowers her pen to pad, scribbling, and frowns. "Oh, dear, Dahlia. I'm sorry to hear that."

I nod. I should be crying right now, but I can't summon a single fucking tear. Or maybe I shouldn't. I know it must look odd, but I can't help it. "Shot in the back of his head twice." I hate how flat my words sound, I could be talking about a piece of trash off the street.

And that's what he was, I tell myself. *A piece of trash.* But that doesn't make his murder right. And I know it. I just can't bring myself to care. I bite my thumbnail, just trying to think straight.

Sandra shakes her head, anguish flashing in her eyes. "That's horrible. I'm truly sorry, Dahlia." She sets her pen down on the pad and leans forward. "Was this the uncle who hurt you?" her voice is soft and full of understanding.

I nod my head, brushing the bastard tears away. "Yes, and he's dead now."

"I see. How do you feel about that?"

"I…" I pause, feeling a weight on my chest, "I feel like I'm somewhat responsible for his death."

Sandra writes something down on her notepad and then looks up at me, her face twisted with curiosity. "Why is that?"

I shrug while shaking my head. Of course I can't tell her everything, but I feel like admitting a partial truth will help me deal with my guilt. "I just do."

Sandra scribbles several lines and then focuses her kind eyes on me, compassion flashing in them. "You can't blame yourself for your uncle's death, Dahlia. It's not healthy."

I shake my head. "Yes, I can. It's because of me he's dead."

Sandra frowns at the conviction in my voice. "Why do you say that?"

"I don't know, I just feel responsible for it in some way." I choke on my words. "But I don't feel bad about it," I admit. "Except for the guilt I feel about not caring, I feel kind of relieved actually. Like, I'm totally happy he's dead." The silence that follows presses down upon me, and I cringe. I hate how that makes me sound, but I can't help it. It's the truth. I look over at Sandra and she's watching me, sitting very still. I wonder what's going on in her head. "Does that make me a bad person?"

Sandra scribbles more notes down on her notepad before

looking back up at me. "Considering what he did to you, no. Not at all." She pauses as if thinking about how to formulate a question. "But now that he's dead, do you think his death will help you?" She pauses again, but I know exactly what she means. "It's important I document the impact that it has on you."

Hugging my knees to myself, I shake my head. "No. I can't believe I'm saying this, but I think I finally was able to let that all go." That same guilt comes back over me, but I push it away. I hate the fact that I'm happy about my uncle being dead, but I can't help myself.

"I see."

I cover my face with my hands as I lean forward crying. *It's because of Lucian. It's all because of him.*

"Dahlia," Sandra's soft voice prods me as she rises from her seat, the sounds accompanying my sobs.

He killed him for me. My heart clenches. I'm a horrible person for loving him for that. That's truly what I feel. It's so fucked up.

Her small hands rub soothing circles on my back. "Have you been able to talk to your partner about this?" she asks me in a small voice. "Lucian?"

I nod my head, wiping under my eyes and reaching for the Kleenex in her hand.

"Do you think you'll be able to confide in him?" she asks. I don't know. My heart squeezes with pain. This is so real. It's so much to take in. I love him. I know I love him, and I can't bear the thought of him leaving me. The contract is over, but I'm not signing another. I want him. I want a commitment. I need it. I need *him*.

CHAPTER 29

LUCIAN

I gave her a chance to come back to me on her own, and she didn't. I'm not going to wait. I refuse to.

The thirty days are over, we have no contract. This is just me and her.

I check my phone one last time before grabbing my keys and opening the door. I swing it open and my heart stops as I stare back at Dahlia. Her eyes are red-rimmed and her hair is a mess.

She came back to me. I'm still in the doorway as she looks up at me with uncertainty. I can't believe she's here. My heart thuds in my chest as she brushes her hair behind her ears and parts her lips.

"Lucian," she says and her voice is soft.

"You came back."

She visibly swallows and takes in a sharp breath. I open the door wider and step to the side. I still can't believe she's here. I thought I'd have to drag her back here. I'm hesitant to think anything positive though. She's obviously not well. And we need to set ground rules. We need to make sure we're on the same page.

She walks in slowly, her hands gripping the strap of her purse. This is either going to go one of two ways. Either she's here to end it, or she's here to stay. And if she's staying, I'm never letting her go.

Her heels click, the sound reverberating off the walls of the foyer as I close the door.

"I'm struggling, Lucian." She turns to face me, still tightly gripping the strap.

I know she is, but everything is going to be alright. "Talk to me, treasure; I want to help you."

She takes in a shaky breath, finally putting her purse down on the table and walking toward me. I open my arms and she walks into my embrace freely. I breathe easy, feeling her pressed against me. Knowing she wants to be held by me. I kiss her hair as she nuzzles her cheek against my chest.

"I'm sorry I made you feel like you had to leave," I apologize. "What I did was something that needed to be done. It wasn't meant to hurt you or to make you afraid of me."

She nods her head in my chest, but she's quiet. I just need her to open up. I need to know what she's thinking.

"I don't want you to leave again. I need you to stay, treasure."

"I don't want to leave, I want you," she whispers into my chest.

"Forgive me." My voice is pained. If I had to do it all over again, I still would've killed him. I know I would have.

"It's not about forgiveness. I think... I love you, Lucian. And that scares the hell out of me." Her confession breaks the wall of insecurity between us. I breathe easily, holding her closer to me and rewarding her honesty with a sweet kiss. My lips mold to hers and I pour my passion into the kiss, needing her to feel it. My hands travel along her body, wanting to claim every inch, but she pulls away slightly, breathing heavily with her eyes closed.

I can feel a but coming. I blink the lust-filled haze away and wait for more. *Just tell me what you need, treasure. I'll give you anything.*

"I'm not okay right now, and all I want is you, but it's not the same for you..."

I pull away from her with my brows pinched. "What do you mean it's not the same for me? You don't think I want you? I've given you everything I can. I don't want to lose you."

"It's just. The contract-" The fucking contract. Just hearing her bring it up makes me snap. I don't care about it. I don't want anything in between us. My blood heats, and all I want to do is show her how much she means to me.

"Fuck the contract! Just don't leave me!" I stare deep into

her eyes, feeling the emotions consuming me. I'm just as raw and vulnerable as she is. "I love you, Dahlia. I want you, and I'll do whatever it takes to keep you."

She takes in a sharp breath, her eyes searching my face. They're filled with hope and doubt.

I need to erase that doubt. I can handle anything but that. I want her passion; I want her heart. I want her everything.

"I love you and I can't let you go," I whisper as I pull her close to me, crushing her small body against mine and molding my lips to hers.

She pulls away from me, and I don't want to let her go. I don't want to break the kiss and lose her.

My eyes are closed as the warmth from our breath comes between our lips, but her body stays pressed against mine. My hands slip up the back of her shirt, feeling her soft skin against mine, keeping her close to me.

"Let me love you forever," I say softly. That's all I want. It's all I need. "Don't leave me again."

"Never. I'll never leave." A weight lifts off my chest as I crash my lips against hers again, needing to feel her. Needing to show her what she means to me.

"I love you, Lucian." Her words make my eyes slowly open and I stare into those beautiful hazel eyes.

"I love you, treasure."

EPILOGUE

LUCIAN

I love that collar around her neck. *My collar.* The gold and diamonds belong there, letting everyone know she's a treasure. *My treasure.*

What's better is how much she loves wearing it. She loves being mine. That's all she wants, and that's something I can always give her. Every day that passes I want her more.

"Are you ready for the show?" I ask my treasure as the waitress collects our empty dinner plates. We've been coming here more often. Club X. It's definitely helping her to learn how Dominants and Submissives are equals in their partnership. The show tonight will really bring that to light.

Her eyes still light up with awe at everything the club has to offer. She's certainly not a voyeur, but when the lights dim and the curtains open, she always asks to climb in my lap. She knows my fingers will travel right where she needs them as we watch. My lips are at her neck. My dick is already hardening. *Soon.*

Isaac invited us to see the show tonight.

He'll be on the stage tonight, but it's not with his Submissive. He's yet to collar her, or rather, she hasn't been willing to let him collar her. It's been nearly a month of them finding each other's limits within the club's boundaries. No Dom has gone near her since they've started their play. But there's still no collar around her neck. She submits for the shows and in the playrooms. She lets him take her to the private rooms. But it ends once she leaves the club, and she's yet to accept any commitment.

I don't understand the dynamic, but it's not my place to question it.

Dahlia breathes in deep, setting her spoon down on the dessert plate. "I'm really excited." She's hardly eaten. It must be her nerves.

"Stop worrying."

She's been letting the stress of going to my sister's party get to her. Christmas is only a week away and I know she's anxious. They hit it off last week when we went to dinner. We even got Italian water ice afterward, despite the cold temps. Both of them got lemon, of course. My treasure has nothing to worry about. Anna loves her already, for showing me I can love again. I'll always have my sister, and now with treasure it feels more like a complete family. I'll never be able to let the rest of my family in, but I'm finally at peace with that.

I take her small hand in mine and turn it over, kissing her wrist. I close my eyes and hum at her soft touch.

"I love you, treasure," I say and kiss her wrist again. It's her left hand and I know I'm going to be putting my ring there soon. I want everyone to know she belongs to me.

"I love you, too," she says sweetly, leaning in and kissing me on the lips. I can feel the eyes of other couples on us.

"Settle down, treasure," I warn her, nipping her bottom lip. She smiles sweetly and obeys. She's still the perfect Submissive. Even when she doesn't think we're playing. I'm still not sure she quite understands, but she trusts me and that's what matters. The trust between us is the only thing that matters.

ABOUT THE AUTHORS

Thank you so much for reading our co-written novel. We hope you loved reading it as much as we loved writing it!

For more information on the books we have published, bonus scenes and more visit our websites.

More by Willow Winters
www.willowwinterswrites.com/books

More by Lauren Landish
www.laurenlandish.com